A Dope Boy's Queen 2

Lock Down Publications and
Ca$h Presents
A Dope Boy's Queen 2
A Novel by **Aryanna**

A Dope Boy's Queen 2

Lock Down Publications
P.O. Box 944
Stockbridge, Ga 30281

Visit our website
www.lockdownpublications.com

Copyright 2020 by Aryanna
A Dope Boy's Queen 2

All rights reserved. No part of this book may be reproduced in any form or by electronic or mechanical means, including information storage and retrieval systems without permission in writing from the publisher, except by a reviewer who may quote brief passages in review.
First Edition October 2020
Printed in the United States of America

This is a work of fiction. Names, characters, places, and incidents either are products of the author's imagination or are used fictitiously. Any similarity to actual events or locales or persons, living or dead, is entirely coincidental.

Lock Down Publications
Like our page on Facebook: **Lock Down Publications** @
www.facebook.com/lockdownpublications.ldp
Cover design and layout by: **Dynasty Cover Me**
Book interior design by: **Shawn Walker**
Edited by: **Kiera Northington**

Aryanna

Stay Connected with Us!

Text **LOCKDOWN** to 22828 to stay up-to-date with new releases, sneak peeks, contests and more…

Submission Guideline.

Submit the first three chapters of your completed manuscript to ldpsubmissions@gmail.com, subject line: Your book's title. The manuscript must be in a .doc file and sent as an attachment. The document should be in Times New Roman, double-spaced and in size 12 font. Also, provide your synopsis and full contact information. If sending multiple submissions, they must each be in a separate email.

Have a story but no way to send it electronically? You can still submit to LDP/Ca$h Presents. Send in the first three chapters, written or typed, of your completed manuscript to:

LDP: Submissions Dept
P.O. Box 944
Stockbridge, Ga 30281

DO NOT send original manuscript. Must be a duplicate.

Provide your synopsis and a cover letter containing your full contact information.

Thanks for considering LDP and Ca$h Presents.

DEDICATION

This book is dedicated to Izzy and Destiny because young love is beautiful.

ACKNOWLEDGEMENTS

I give all glory to God for bringing me this far, and never leaving me, even when I left him. I have to thank my Sunshine Bear for coming back into my life. You and I have been through A LOT, but without it we wouldn't be who we are. Nothing describes our relationship better than the word LOVE. I love you, lover you, want you, and need you. This next phase will be more special than either of us imagined. I have to thank the next generation; Aryanna, Micaela, and Izzy. I love you all individually and as a whole. Destiny, Izzy wanted you to know that you're the love of her life. Make sure that you don't hurt my baby! I have to thank my fans for continuing to support me. I hope you will join me in the next phase of my journey as I step behind the scenes. I have to thank my family for being dysfunctional and helping to shape me. I have to thank my LDP family for the love and loyalty you continue to give. I appreciate you for real. I have to thank the people who have touched my life because I've come to understand that God uses many hands to do his work. I wanna give a shout out to all the real goons that I know. An intelligent goon is a rare breed, and an endangered species. Stay woke. I gotta shout out all the fuck niggas worldwide! It's too many of you to mention by name, but you're all cut from the same cloth, which means the same fate awaits you. Good luck with that. Oh, and I cannot forget the females who be on fuck shit too because you all DON'T get away. Tabitha Whitlock I'm talking about you! Lol. You're a silly bitch, and that's OK because I don't mind paying for my entertainment. Good luck in life. Special shout out to TEDDY BUTLER! Stay out of trouble and come home! I have to thank any and all haters for keeping me motivated. I take no days off because of you, and you'll never know how much I appreciate you. I gotta give a BIG SHOUT OUT to an author by the name of CYN. This is

A Dope Boy's Queen 2

a family business now baby, so make me proud. If I've forgotten anyone, I'm sorry, but its 2am and I've been up for 24 hours. I love you, though!

Aryanna

Chapter 1

The sight of a man's head exploding a few feet from me should've broken the spell of the trance I was under, but it didn't. The roar of gunfire should've made me duck for cover, or try to grab my own gun, but neither of those things happened. All I could do in this moment was look at Phillisa, and silently curse her past the pits of hell.

"Move!" Mo yelled, pushing me out of the way and knocking me to the floor.

The sound of bullets hitting the wall behind me in the spot where I'd just been standing told me she'd saved my life, and that kind of jarred me out of my shock. I quickly scrambled to grab the gun I'd dropped on the floor, but when I went to turn it on Phillisa, she was nowhere to be seen.

"Did you hit her, Mo?"

"No, her punk ass help caught the bullets meant for her," she replied, still dumping shots at the wall of bodies trying to close in on us from across the room.

Campa's office wasn't small, but it was only so big which meant that we were all shooting fish in a barrel, hoping to hit something. I could hear shots coming from behind me and that Fatz had stepped into the room from his post outside the door.

"Spread out!" I yelled, diving behind one of the two leather couches that occupied the space we were trying to turn into a funeral home.

Mo took the opposite couch, and Fatz followed her lead. I wasted no time sticking my gun around the couch and letting that motherfucker bark loudly. By the time I heard the click of my gun going empty, there was a roar from behind me that would've made any lion proud. I looked back to see Vontrell stepping through the door, with an automatic Mossberg shotgun resting on his hip.

"This is how we do it in the shore, nigga!" he yelled.

The sudden screams coming from either Phillisa's or Campa's men were the sweetest music to my ears, and I found myself smiling while reloading. I wasted no time hopping back into the gunfight, and by the time the last body dropped, I could hear the sounds of more shooting going on throughout the compound.

"Where are they?" I asked, quickly searching the room for Phillisa and Campa.

"I-I don't see them," Mo replied, kicking bodies to turn them over so she could see their faces.

"They couldn't have gotten away, there's only one door they could go through and we were blocking it," I stated, becoming more frustrated.

"What's that?" Fatz asked.

I followed his gaze to the bookshelf at the back of Campa's office, at first not seeing what he was saying. I kept staring though, until I realized that the bookshelf was actually pulled away from the wall, and there was a sliver of light shining into the office.

"Mother-fucker!" I exclaimed angrily, moving swiftly to the hidden passageway.

I had to put all my weight into pushing open the hidden door, but I still didn't hesitate to pass through it in search of my enemies.

"Wait for me," Mo said from behind me.

I didn't stop or slow down though. I made my way down the winding staircase as fast as I could while making sure to keep my gun out in front of me. The further I went down, the softer the sound of gunshots got, but I was still ready for anything to happen. Finally, after what felt like a million steps, my feet came into contact with flat ground, causing me to pause and wait for both Fatz and Mo. The lighting was beyond dim, making it necessary to take the time to let my eyes adjust to what I couldn't see.

"Which way?" Mo asked.

I looked at the entrances to three paths before us, wondering who in the hell built this maze and what type of fuckery awaited at the end of the wrong tunnel.

"I-I don't know, I've never been down here before. I didn't even know this shit existed," I replied honestly.

"Split up," Fatz said, raising his gun and heading in the direction of the tunnel to his right.

A Dope Boy's Queen 2

Mo went to the left, which left me with the one straight up the middle. I followed their lead, taking my time to walk so I could hear anything out of the ordinary. The further I moved the more the silence wrapped itself around me, making me feel extremely uneasy, but I pushed on by sheer force of will. There was no telling how deep these tunnels were, or if they were boobytrapped, but I kept catching the faint smell of water.

At first, I thought I was tripping, but when my tunnel suddenly came alive with the sounds of an engine in the distance, I took off at a dead sprint. I tripped over my own feet but managed to use the slippery wall to prevent going face-first into the rocky floor. I still didn't slow down or pause in my hot pursuit of the engine I could hear clearly now.

"Mo!" I screamed.

I knew there was a chance she couldn't hear me, and I started to fire a shot from my pistol, because she would automatically come running for that. The problem with that was I would be warning my enemies of my presence. I dared not to do that, so I continued running as fast as I dared to. When I rounded the corner, I spotted an opening in the tunnels and the sight of waves moving in the distance. I had no choice except to slow down, because I didn't wanna run headlong into a fast-moving bullet. I could still hear the engine though as I crept up on the opening, but by the time I got close enough to shoot at the fast-moving boat, it was speeding away.

"Fuck!" I growled through clenched teeth, shaking with pure rage.

I stood there and watched the boat until it disappeared from my vision, wishing with all my might that I could drag it back to me.

"Did she get away?" Mo asked from behind me.

"Not just her, but Campa's bitch ass too," I replied disgustedly.

"So, what do we do now?" Fatz asked.

I paused for a moment to contemplate my options, before turning around to face both of them in the barely shining light.

"We kill everybody left alive upstairs, and then we hunt them to the ends of the Earth."

Fatz nodded his agreement first, but Morano was slow to second the motion, before turning to lead the way from which we came. It took us five minutes to make it back upstairs and to no surprise, the sound of gunshots was still ringing loudly. We wasted no time stepping out of the office and following the sounds, shooting anyone we didn't know along the way. It took us no longer than fifteen minutes to declare Campa's mansion captured by enemy forces, and when that was done, we reconvened in what used to be his office.

"Don't you think we need to be getting out of here?" J5 asked.

"No, I don't. This house and everything in it, belongs to me now and I'll be treating it as such. If you don't want your piece of the pie, you're free to leave out the front door. No hard feelings," I replied, sitting behind Campa's desk.

"You can't just steal a whole house like that," Mo said, looking at me like I'd lost my mind.

"Of course I can, Mo. I'm a lawyer who knows about acquiring estates from fugitives, and when I'm done, that motherfucker and his precious daughter will be wanted in every country known to man," I said.

"I like the way you do business," Fatz said smiling.

"I second that," J5 said.

"Good. J5, I want you and your team to round up all the bodies for disposal, and I'll call my guy. Vontrell, if he needs any help, I want you and your people to help him. Red Gunz, I want you and your people positioned around the compound to make sure we don't get any surprise visitors. Any questions?" I asked, looking around the room at the people I'd addressed.

No one spoke, so I nodded my head to let them know that would be all.

"Snow, I get that you're angry, but do you really think it's wise to take over Campa's house?" Mo asked.

"It's definitely wise, and that's only the half of it," Fatz said before I could respond.

Mo and I turned our eyes on him, with the same look of confusion as to who asked him to speak for me.

"Before either of you bite my head off, I want you to follow me so I can show you something," he said. Without waiting for acknowledgement of our compliance, he headed towards the hidden door to the tunnels we'd just came out of.

I got up from behind the desk, grabbed Mo by the hand and pulled her behind me. We made our way back down into the hidden cave-like atmosphere, but instead of going down the tunnels Mo and I had been in, Fatz led the way down his tunnel. It was darker than I remembered, but instead of straining my eyes to see, I pulled my phone out and turned it on to light up the night. It only took a few moments to see what Fatz had been talking about upstairs.

"Hoooolllllyyyyy shit!" Mo exclaimed, pushing past me to get a better look at what laid in front of us.

From floor to ceiling, the tunnels were at least twelve to fifteen feet high, with a curved arch at the top. Stacked from floor to ceiling were pallets you might find in any supermarket, but instead of being loaded down with food, they were loaded with neatly stacked white bricks.

"H-how much coke is that?" Mo asked, turning to face me.

"A lot," I replied, moving closer so I could get a better look.

"You really had no idea, huh?" Fatz asked, looking directly at me.

"Absolutely none, but I'm not surprised, because Campa is nothing if not unpredictable. If I'm looking at this right, and I might not be because I don't know how far back this tunnel reaches, but this easily has to be a few metric tons of coke."

"How-how much is that worth, Claudette?" Mo asked in awe.

"Enough to kill behind, so I need you both to understand this just went next level. We won't just be hunting Campa and Phillisa, we'll be hunted by Campa's supplier and his associates," I said.

"I figured that much, but that could work to our advantage," Fatz replied.

"It could work in our favor to lure the devil to our door?" Mo asked, pushing me aside so she could move closer to Fatz.

"Yeah. It could, bae, because the head snake coming for us will undoubtedly lead to Campa's location, and his daughter's too if she stays with him. I ain't scared to take on anybody because at the end of the day, they bleed just like us," Fatz said.

"And you're still willing to die for this?" I asked, gesturing towards the large stockpiles.

"I'm still willing to die for my lady, and the fact that they came for us first," he replied.

"Fatz, you know how I feel about you but this, this is gonna be different than anything we've faced together," Mo said.

He stepped away from the dope and went to stand beside his woman. I thought he would express his love for her the way that only he could, but instead of words, he simply wrapped his arms around her and pulled her to his chest. Even in the dark, I could see the comfort on her face, and it made me yearn for my husband in a way I hadn't in a while. The ache of loss never dissipated when it came to Zion, but I hadn't really had time to focus on it since my life had spun out of control. The sudden thought of Phillisa flashed across my mind, and the ache of the loss I'd felt turned into an anger that I'd never known.

"Mo? Do-do you think she was telling the truth?" I asked.

I could see the sympathy on both of their faces instantly, and it made me feel some type of way. Claudette Snow didn't accept pity from anyone.

"Don't answer that, we've still got work to do, and now ain't the time for this extra sensitive ass shit."

"Claudette, I—"

I didn't wait on her to finish her sentence before turning on my heels and making my way back upstairs. I could hear both her and Fatz moving behind me, but I walked fast enough that a conversation was impossible. As soon as I was back in the office, I got on the phone and started to call in some favors I'd amassed over the years. Those that knew me knew I was formidable in both the streets and the courtroom, so my list of friends were the real movers and shakers in life.

My first call was to a judge friend of mine who dealt with estates and seized property, but I was counting on him being smart enough to know I was the wrong enemy to battle in court of law.

My next call was to a former client that I'd help beat a vehicular manslaughter charge a year ago, because he owned a funeral home and I needed a place to get rid of the bodies. Once that was taken care of, I contacted the people I distributed to, and let them know about a special I was running on coke. In every area I knew Campa was operating in, I dropped the price so drastically, he would have to give his product away to get rid of it. I sat back with a satisfied smile on my face when I was done and started to plan the next series of moves in mind.

"I can smell the wood burning," Mo said, sitting up in the chair she'd been slouched in.

"Just thinking of a master plan," I replied.

"Whatever it is, we're in," Fatz stated from his seat beside Mo.

"It's gonna get ugly," I warned.

"Tell us something we don't know," Mo said smiling.

Aryanna

Chapter 2

One Week Later

"Have you been asleep yet?"

I looked up from the frying pan in my hand, to find Ashlei standing in the middle of the kitchen staring at me.

"Huh?"

"You heard me, Snow. You've been standing there looking at that damn pan for at least the five minutes I've been standing here watching you. So, when was the last time you actually slept, sweetie?" she asked, moving closer to me.

Her question was borderline annoying the fuck out of me, but even more than that, I was getting pissed that I couldn't readily remember the answer to her question.

"I sleep when I'm tired, Ashlei, don't worry. What's up with you though?"

"Don't try to change the subject, bitch. We're all concerned with how you've become obsessed with finding them, and—"

"I'm not obsessed, I'm just focused and I'm not about to apologize for that," I replied defensively, throwing the pan in the sink and storming out of the room.

It had been my intention to get out of the house and get some air, but when I opened the door, I ran smack into one of Red Gunz's men blocking my way.

"Move," I demanded.

"I'm sorry, Mrs. Snow, but I can't do that."

"You wanna repeat that?" I asked, pulling the black Glock .23 from the small of my back, and letting it rest against my thigh.

"I mean no disrespect, ma'am, but I've got orders to follow, and I was told not to let you leave this house."

"And who the fuck gave you those orders?" I asked in disbelief.

"I did."

I turned around at the sound of Mo's voice to find her standing shoulder-to-shoulder with Ashlei and Fatz. My anger came so fast and white hot, I thought I might spontaneously combust right where

Aryanna

I stood. Instead, I turned back to the guard standing on my doorstep, raised my gun, and shot him once between the eyes.

"Let that be a lesson to all of you, because I hate to repeat myself," I said, tucking my gun away as I stepped over his dead body en route to my car.

"There are more where he came from, Snow, so you'll never make it off this property without being restrained eventually." Mo's words stopped me cold and forced me to turn back and face them.

"Don't play with me, and that warning is for all of you," I stated forcefully.

"No one is playing, Snow. We're all in this together and therefore, we have to look out for one another. This is us looking out for you," Mo said.

I pulled my gun back out while staring at the three of them and trying to decide who to shoot first. I didn't expect looks of fear, I just expected them to know how serious I was. When Mo started moving towards me, I tightened my grip on my pistol, but I didn't raise it. Yet.

"Do you love me, Snow?" she asked softly.

"That ain't got shit to do with this," I said.

"Of course it does, because it's love that has us standing here right now. It's love that has bred the loyalty we all have for each other. And it'll be love that allows us to die for one another. I know you're hurting, baby, but you ain't lost sight of that," she said.

By now we were standing toe to toe, and I could see the love in her eyes. I also saw the pain she was feeling, and I knew it was my pain that was hurting her because of the love she'd just spoke about. Seeing all of this made my heart beat faster, and I could feel the tears prickling my eyes. I didn't stop her from taking the gun from my hand, or from taking my hand and leading me back inside the house. I could feel the tears streaming down my face, but the pain gripping me was so powerful that I didn't bother to wipe them away.

Ashlei grabbed me by my other hand, and we walked upstairs side by side. In the time since I'd relocated back to my house from my newly acquired mansion, I had yet to step foot inside my bedroom. Normally, I enjoyed the time in my sanctuary because everything around me reminded me of Zion. After hearing about Phillisa's affair, I barely wanted to remember my cheating ass husband's name, let alone anything else about him.

When we walked in the room, I just stopped and stared at the bed. Part of me was remembering the love we made, while the other part was wondering if Zion was fucking Phillisa here when I wasn't around.

"Are you okay, Snow? You're shaking," Ashlei asked, squeezing my hand tighter.

"I-I'm fine."

Despite my words, I still didn't move from the spot I was standing in.

"Mo, I need to ask a favor of you," I said.

"Anything," she replied without hesitation.

I looked at her briefly, before turning my eyes back on the bed in front of me.

"I wanna be fucked," I stated.

"I'll leave you two alone, so you can—"

"No, Ashlei, I want you here too, and—"

"And what?" Mo asked when I stopped talking.

I hesitated for a second, giving careful consideration to what I was about to say next.

"I want Fatz in here too," I said, looking at her again.

I caught the instant flash of some emotion, but it was gone before I could identify it. She didn't respond right away, she just stared at me with a blank look. When she let go of my hand and backed out of the room, I felt like I'd gone too far and maybe hurt our relationship with my request. That hadn't been my intention, but when I turned to follow her so I could explain, I found her coming right back into the room with Fatz in tow.

"Snow, you know I love you, and you know how much I love Fatz…so there are gonna be some rules to this shit. There will be no kissing whatsoever. He's putting a condom on, because he ain't cumming in nobody except me. Ashlei, if you're in this then you're all the way in it, but this is still a one-time thing, so—"

"Wait, wait, wait, what the hell are you talking about?" Fatz asked, looking a little more than confused.

"Are you sure, Mo?" I asked, staring at her intently.

"Sure about what?" Fatz asked, looking at us.

"Yeah, I'm sure."

The look on Mo's face matched her words, making me hold my hand out to her. When she reached for me and our fingers touched, I pulled her into my arms. Our first kiss was soft and sweet, almost innocent in a way, but it got deeper quick. The way her hands roamed my body brought it to life instantly, and I could feel my pussy start to throb. As our tongues love tapped each other's, we were undressing each other, until there was nothing between us but the air in our lungs. When her hand slid in between my thighs, and her fingers gently parted my pussy lips, I stopped breathing.

"It's okay, I got you," she whispered into my mouth.

I opened my legs a little wider, and the moment I felt two of her fingers slip inside me, I breathed again. The way she moved in a clockwise motion, had me holding onto her tightly and breathing hard within seconds. I knew if I didn't fight, I'd be lost long before this was all over, so I gave her some of the same treatment she was giving me.

"Damn you're t-tight," I said, pushing my fingers inside her hot pussy forcefully.

"Look who-who's talking," she replied, slightly out of breath.

"Whatttttt is happening?" Fatz whispered.

It wasn't my intention to ignore him and Ashlei, but Mo had me lost in the moment. I pulled back enough to look deeply into Mo's hazel eyes.

"You take her, and I'll take him," I said.

"I'll meet you in the bed," she replied.

I kissed her again quickly, and we pulled ourselves apart. When I turned my gaze on Fatz, I could tell he was less confused, and more curious now.

"I hope this dick is as good as advertised," I said, stepping over to him and pulling his shorts straight to the floor.

His response was to smile at me with pride, before stepping out of his shorts, picking me up by my waist and carrying me to my bed. He didn't sit me down gently, he tossed me like a rag doll and that turned me on more. There was no time wasted when it came to him shedding his remaining clothes, and before I knew it, he was on top of me and his weight was pinning me to the bed.

"How do you want it?" he asked.

"Rough," I replied honestly.

"Show me," he demanded.

I quickly rolled him on his back and climbed on top of him.

"Wait," Mo said.

I looked back at her and saw she had a condom in her hand. I scooted back enough for her to get in between us, so she could roll the latex down his beautiful black dick. Seeing it throbbing and bobbing had my pussy twitching wildly. Some of it was fear, but I wasn't gonna let that stop me. Once she had his shaft completely covered, she put her whole mouth on the tip of his dick, and slowly slid her lips around and down it until every inch of the condom had vanished.

"Damn bitch, no gag reflex," I said chuckling softly.

When she started to hum, he started to moan. It was fascinating watching her move with a dancer's grace as her head came up and down. I could feel his legs start to tremble, and she must've too because she unwrapped her lips from around him.

"Get on it," she said, smacking me on the ass.

I didn't need to be told twice because I was like a track star out of the starter's block. I knew I was supposed to use caution, but before I could stop myself, I was suspended in the air and coming down fast on the dick.

"Oh God," I moaned softly.

I bit my lip to keep my pride intact, but I didn't move because of the pleasurable pain shooting through my body. Once I gathered my courage, I started out slowly until I felt comfortable in my own skin. Once I could slide down the dick without knocking the wind out of me, I knew I was ready to fuck. I could tell by the look on his face that he was enjoying being up in this good-good, but this was only the beginning. I grabbed ahold of the headboard and used it as leverage, going from zero to a thousand on the dick.

"You better ride that nigga!" Ashlei said.

I didn't look back at her, but I absolutely took her advice. I could feel him throbbing all the way up in my stomach, and it was a feeling I'd missed with every fiber of my being. My pussy was screaming at the invasion of something so big, but every time I rose until just the tip was in me, it screamed to be invaded again.

"Sl-slow down, Snow," he panted, holding onto my hips.

I put one hand on his throat and the other over his mouth, and I popped my pussy faster.

His moans were loud, but when I started moving on just the head of his dick, he started bucking beneath me and yelling.

"Damn, that's sexy," Mo said softly.

I was surprised that when I looked to my left, Mo was right there leaning on the bed. I thought she was watching us, until I saw Ashlei eating her pussy from the back. Mo's eyes were already glassy with her building climax, and the sight of it turned me on more. I didn't concentrate on the nigga beneath me fucking me, I watched Mo and Ashlei instead. When Mo closed her eyes and I heard the low growl in her throat, I knew she was cumming, and that pushed me beneath the waters of orgasm.

"Ohhhhhh, fuck!" I exclaimed loudly.

I was holding onto Fatz for dear life, squeezing him with both my pussy muscles and the hand around his throat. I thought I had it under control, but the harder I came, the faster I was overcome by emotions. When I suddenly tasted salty tears in my mouth, I stopped moving on the dick and got up.

"S-Snow, you good?" Mo asked.

I couldn't find the words to answer, so I didn't say shit as I made a hasty escape to the bathroom. Before I could close the door, Mo was right there pushing her way inside.

"It's okay, sweetie, it's okay," she said, pulling me into her arms as she kicked the door closed.

I clung to her, and let the tears fall while trying to suppress the screams clawing at my throat. As furious as I was at Zion and

A Dope Boy's Queen 2

Phillisa's betrayal, my heart still hurt over what I'd just done. Part of me felt like I'd just destroyed the sanctity of my marriage, even though I knew that was foolish.

"You didn't do anything wrong, Snow. You're a young woman who deserves to live, instead of being trapped in the past."

"I-I know, b-but—"

"No buts, Snow. You deserve happiness! I won't speak ill of Zion, but you know that shit he did was foul, and I know it hurt you. The best way to get over it is to get back to living all parts of your life. I'm with you, bae."

I wasn't sure what argument I would put forward, but I knew she'd have an answer for it, so I didn't bother. I hated to cry, because it made me feel like such a weak bitch, but I needed to cry this time. I needed the freedom that came with tears, and I knew Mo wouldn't judge me for that. I stayed locked in her arms, crying until I felt somewhat better. When I pulled back and looked at her face, I saw silent tears streaming down her face.

"Thank you, Anastasia."

"If you wanna thank me, then don't use my first name, it makes me feel old."

I chuckled softly before kissing her on the lips.

"I got you, Mo."

"And I got you right back, bitch. Now let's go have some fun."

I nodded in agreement before turning to open the door. I took in the sight in front of me and suddenly, my pussy was wet again. Ashlei was on top of Fatz riding him reverse cowgirl style, while holding her ankles.

"I never knew she was that flexible," I said, impressed.

"Me either, and she's taking the dick like it ain't nothing."

The sounds of our voices made Ashlei turn her head in our direction, but her looming orgasm had her speechless.

"Ahhhhhhh!" she screamed, shaking harder than any wet dog I'd ever seen.

"Is your pussy wet?" I asked, looking over my shoulder at Mo.

"Hell yeah!" I took her by the hand and led her back to bed.

23

Aryanna

We didn't interrupt Ashlei's moment, choosing instead to join the fun. I popped my tittie in Fatz' mouth while Mo went back to playing with my pussy. It only took me moments to cum, and this time I didn't cry. That was all I needed to release me from my demons, at least for this moment in time.

Once Ashlei finished cumming, Mo got on top of her nigga, and I sat on Ashlei's face and rode her like I had Fatz. After my third or fourth orgasm, I lost track of reality. Everybody was fucking everybody, and it was beautiful.

Chapter 3

"What-what time is it?" Ashlei asked breathlessly.

"It's like three p.m.," I mumbled, rolling from in between her legs and onto my back.

"Mo, we gotta go to work," she said with obvious regret.

"Can you walk, bitch?" I asked Ashlei.

"Barely. What about you, Mo?"

"I'm used to the punishment my baby puts down, it's you bitches that can't hang."

The sudden and unexpected sound of snoring had all eyes locked on Fatz, who was curled up next to me. I busted out laughing, which made his eyes shoot open like someone had fired a gun.

"It's okay, baby, you just dozed off for a second," Mo said snickering.

"You-you all tried to kill me," he said seriously.

"Nigga, you loved it!" I said laughing.

"I'm not saying I didn't, but damn!"

We all laughed together as we laid side by side on my bed. Despite my slight breakdown earlier, I felt hella relaxed. Sore, but relaxed.

"Come on, bitch," Ashlei said, pulling Mo up off the bed with her.

I knew neither one of them wanted to go to work, but I needed them to. Their position inside the department of corrections, kept our ears to the street in a different way. Plus, it helped when it came to recruiting new soldiers for my army. They got up off the bed, leaving me and Fatz laying there. I waited until I heard the shower come on before speaking.

"Thank you, Fatz."

"For what?"

"Today, this moment, the dick, you choose which one doesn't make you feel used," I said.

"I don't feel used by you, Snow, I feel honored you chose me. I know it wasn't easy, but hopefully it was freeing."

Aryanna

I thought about what he said before replying. "It was freeing. I think that's the best way to describe it."

"Good. I'm here whenever you need me," he offered, smiling genuinely.

"Mo already said this was a one-time thing."

"I think she meant that more so for Ashlei than you, but I'll talk to her and clarify," he said.

I let the thought of fucking him roll around my head for a minute, and when my thoughts shifted to Zion, I pushed the guilt down. I had nothing to feel guilty for, but I definitely had some scores to settle. I got up slowly off the bed and went to take a shower in the guest bedroom. I could've easily gone in the shower with Ashlei and Mo, but I wanted a moment alone with my thoughts.

I stood still under the blistering spray for at least ten minutes before I even reached for the soap. My mind was no longer on the amazing sex I'd just had, it was back on the business of killing. I had every man and woman under my command looking for Phillisa and Campa, but so far no one had seen them. I'd basically taken over Campa's territory and used his product to do it, but that still hadn't brought him out of his hiding spot. It was obvious to me it was gonna take more drastic measures.

My mind was cycling around a crazy idea while I was lathering my body with soap, and by the time I finished bathing, I was convinced about my next move. I quickly dried off once I got out of the shower, and went back to my room to get dressed. I could still hear the shower running in my bathroom, and Fatz was back to snoring, which meant I was basically alone. I hurriedly got dressed, grabbed my gun, and ran from the room.

I made it downstairs and into the garage without anyone stopping me, but I had no idea what awaited me once the door went up. I didn't let that stop me though. I hopped behind the wheel of my Aston Martin, clicked the button to raise the door, and prepared to back up. The sight of Meatrock in my rearview mirror, standing in my way made me pause though. I had a few options, but I was leaning towards the one that involved me shooting him in the legs. I chose to scare him instead, though. I hit the gas pedal hard, making my car rocket backwards. Luckily for Meat, he had quick enough reflexes to jump out of the way.

"Get the fuck in," I said, sliding to a stop next to where he was laying.

I could see his hesitation, but he was smart enough to pull himself up off the ground and get in the car.

"You know you're not supposed to leave the house, right?" he asked.

"I'm grown, Meatrock, so shut up."

"Are you at least gonna tell me where we're going?" he asked.

"The devil's door so I can knock in person."

"What the fuck does that mean?" he asked.

The smile I turned on him made him shake his head, but he knew he was in it with me now. I put my foot down hard on the accelerator and let my V-12 engine eat up the road. The move I had in mind was more than risky, but if I wanted results, I had no other options.

It didn't take long to get out of the wealthy part of the Florida Keys where my house was located, and into the disenfranchised hoods of Little Haiti.

"Who do you know down here?" he asked.

"It might be a friend or a possible enemy, I guess we'll see when we get there."

I could feel the heat of his stare, but I didn't look at him and just kept driving. About thirty minutes after we got into the grimy part of town, I eased my car to a stop in front of a rundown house. I didn't get out though, I turned off the engine, and waited.

"What exactly are we waiting for?" he asked.

"Patience, Meatrock."

Before he could say anything else, three men carrying AK-47's, came from different directions to surround the car.

"Turn the engine off and get out."

I didn't recognize the voice, but I did as I was told and nodded for Meatrock to follow my lead. I moved with deliberate slowness, and kept my hands where they could be seen.

"State your business," the man standing closest to me said.

Aryanna

"I need to speak to Nicki, is she here?" I asked pleasantly.

"Is she expecting you?" he asked.

"Nah, but tell her Claudette Snow is requesting a moment of her time," I said.

The three men looked at each other, before the one standing next to me pulled a radio from his pocket and spoke into it. Silence greeted him at first, and then I heard a voice that I hadn't heard in a few years.

"If that's really Snow out there, I want all of you to shoot her," Nicki said.

"Tell her I have a present for her," I said quickly.

The other two raised their guns, but the closest one to me waved them off.

"Are you really *the* Claudette Snow?" he asked.

The look in his brown eyes told me he'd heard my name somewhere before now, but I didn't know if that was a good thing or not.

"Yeah, I am."

He stared at me for a moment longer before putting the radio back to his lips and relaying my message. Again, Nicki didn't say anything at first, and then I saw the front door to the house open. No one stood there to greet me, but I knew this was my invitation. I gave Meatrock a look, and he followed me up the sidewalk and into the house. The interior was dimly lit, and the smell of good weed permeated the air, pulling us towards the back of the house.

From the outside, one would expect the inside to be rundown and falling apart, but Nicki Davenport didn't get down like that. She was a showstopper, and everything around her had to reflect that. The interior of the house could've been something seen on a movie set with the priceless works of art, sculptures and gold inlay, but this was simply Nicki's sanctuary. Not many people would build one of those in the middle of the ghetto, but Nicki wasn't like many people.

When I rounded the corner, I spotted her sitting at her kitchen table sipping an amber liquid, while caressing her pistol lovingly. When she lifted her gaze to meet my eyes, I knew instantly this shit had the potential to go left. Her usually golden colored eyes were green, and that meant she was already pissed. I took in the language her five foot six, one-hundred-fifty-pound frame was giving me while crossing the kitchen floor to sit across the table from her. I didn't read any aggression, just the open hostility I'd expected to find.

"It's been awhile, Nicki, how have you been?" I asked smiling. Her gun came up immediately and levelled off at my right eye.

"Easy, Nicki, I come in peace."

"If you don't wanna leave in pieces, I suggest you stop playing with me. Now what-the-fuck do you want?" she growled at me.

"I need to find Campa."

"I don't know where the fuck your precious Jefe is, bitch, why don't you try his house!"

"Nah, he ain't there, that's my house now. I own everything in this town that belongs to him," I said smiling.

"Bullshit."

I didn't say anything, I simply looked at her over the barrel of her gun and waited. After a moment's hesitation, she lowered the pistol back to the table, and stared at me with open skepticism.

"You're serious?" she asked.

"You have your ear to the streets, don't you? So, I know you heard about some shit going down last week."

"I thought that was some other fool ass motherfucker trying to take on the almighty empire Jefe built," she replied smiling.

"Nah, it was mutiny, and I'm on my pirate shit."

"Okay, so why come to me for help, Snow? I don't owe you shit, and I don't like your ass."

"Yeah, but you dislike him even more. And I know you've gotten older, but you ain't forgot who helped you once you got excommunicated from our organization."

"Bitch, it was your fault I got the boot!" she yelled angrily.

I didn't flinch, but I could tell Meatrock did, because she immediately swung the gun to him.

"If you shoot him, I'll kill you," I said softly.

Nicki kept the gun pointed at him, but her eyes were on me. I knew she could tell how serious I was despite the obvious disadvantage, and that kept her from pulling the trigger.

"In case you have developed amnesia, it was you who got caught with your hand in the cookie jar," I said.

"I wasn't stealing, I—"

"I know, you were trying to build your own thing, and that's why I didn't kill you. I respected your entrepreneurial spirit, so I left you in a position to eat, instead of eating you my damn self," I said.

I could tell she wanted to argue, but I saw the truth in her eyes. We both knew I was telling the truth because Campa had wanted me to kill her. When you worked for Campa, you didn't get any bright ideas about having your own thing and if you did, you were disloyal.

I should've seen that as a sign of the things to come, but I hadn't been worried about my position being in jeopardy. When I'd looked out for Nicki, I'd told her she didn't owe me shit, and I'd meant that, but we both knew what type of bitch she'd be not to help in this situation.

"So, do you really have a gift for me, or is your guilt trip all you brought?" she asked sarcastically.

"No, I actually do have a proposition for you if you help me. I'm willing to give you large quantities of good dope at reasonable prices, and I'll do it consistently," I said smiling.

"You're offering me a drug pipeline?"

"Is that not enough?" I asked.

"I didn't say that. I just wanted to make sure I understood the offer."

"Well, that's the offer and it comes with all the protections I have. Recently, those have increased dramatically," I said, glancing over my shoulder at Meatrock.

When I turned my eyes back on Nicki, I found her staring at him over my shoulder too, but the look in her eyes was different.

"What is it you need, Snow?" she asked.

"I need to find Campa and his daughter, Phillisa. If they're not in Florida, then they had to use a lot of back channels to get out without me knowing, and you know those channels. Find them for me so I can hunt them."

"Campa has a daughter?" she asked, surprised.

I pulled my phone out of my pocket and pulled up a picture I'd taken of Phillisa during our time together in Columbia. The anger I felt at the moments we'd shared was on my tongue like bad breath. I'd never been so thoroughly played, and I never would be again.

"She's gorgeous," Nicki said.

"And the pussy is good too. So, are you gonna help me or what?" I asked impatiently.

For a moment she just stared at me with her mouth open, but she recovered and passed me my phone back.

"I'll help you, but I want something else," she said.

"What's that, Nicki?"

When her eyes skated past me over my shoulder, I chuckled softly before stepping aside.

"You're up, kid," I said, nodding towards Nicki.

At first, Meatrock looked at me in confusion, but that quickly vanished, and he stepped around me to get to Nicki.

"What can I do for you?" he asked.

"Everything," she replied smiling, as she stood up and took his hand.

I occupied the seat she'd vacated, still chuckling as she led Meatrock away. Within a few minutes, I could hear the sounds of Nicki's moans floating on the air. The intensity built rapidly and before I knew it, her moans had turned to screams. I smiled while picking up the half of a blunt sitting in the ashtray in front of me. I lit it, and thought about how fucked Campa and Phillisa were, courtesy of the fucking Nicki was taking. The irony was comical.

Aryanna

Chapter 4

"Wake your snoring ass up, nigga," I said, smacking Meatrock upside his head.

He immediately jerked upright in the passenger seat of my car, reaching for his gun.

"You better not pull that little motherfucker out on me nigga!"

"You can ask your girl, this motherfucker is far from little," he replied yawning.

"I was talking about your gun, smartass."

"Oh...so was I," he said, laughing.

"Yeah whatever, let's go in here and face the music," I said, opening my door and getting out of the car.

I already knew everybody in my house was gonna be pissed and have something to say, but the move I'd made had yielded results, so I couldn't regret it. Nicki was now an ally, and because she kept her nimble fingers in so many pies, was bound to get the results I was after. I knew all I needed to do was explain this to my team, and shit would be all good.

It was amazing what making progress could do for the human psyche, because I actually found myself yawning as I unlocked my front door. It didn't register to me that it was dark in the foyer until the light suddenly flicked on, and I was blinded by the brightness. Before I could adjust to the change, I caught sight of a swift movement, and the next thing I knew I was flying backwards into Meatrock.

"Bitch, have you lost your mind?" I yelled, holding my jaw where I'd been punched.

Mo didn't say shit, but I could tell by the way she was advancing on me that she wasn't done. I pushed off Meatrock and put my hands up fast enough to block her next two punches.

"I'm telling you now, Mo, you better stop the dumb shit," I said.

The look in her eyes told me that my words were falling on deaf ears. The bitch was on a mission. I pulled out my gun, tossed it to Meatrock, and went on offense. I faked a left jab and caught her flush on the chin with a right hook that wobbled her knees. Before

I could advance on her, she recovered and was coming at me with a steady barrage of punches. I absorbed the body blows so I could protect my face, but when she landed a fierce uppercut to my sternum, I knew I'd fucked up. In my mind, I was gonna whoop this bitch but in reality, I was fighting to breathe.

I saw her right hook coming, but my pride wouldn't let me stay there. I could feel myself tapping into all the hurt and anger I kept bottled up, and it was like adding nitrogen to kerosene. This time when I advanced on Mo, I wasn't looking at her like a friend, sister, or lover. She was my opponent. I raised my hands in preparation to throw a combination, but I saw an opening and decided to take it instead. I kicked her squarely in her chest before she could block me or get out of the way. By the time her back hit the ground, I was on her motherfucking chest, swinging left and right hooks at her face.

"Stop, Snow... Stop!" Ashlei yelled, pulling me backwards, and wrapping her arms and legs around me.

I struggled mightily to get free, but Ashlei had me wrapped up tighter than a boa.

"Get off me now!" I growled, still struggling.

"No! You had this shit coming, and you know it," Ashlei said, tightening her grip.

It only took a few moments for me to realize that continuing to fight against the lock Ashlei had on me was pointless. The bitch had wrestled in high school.

"I didn't have a goddamn thing coming. I'm grown, and I can go where I wanna go. Now, get the fuck off me," I said angrily.

"Let her go," Mo said, climbing to her feet.

I halfway expected her to advance on me while I was helpless on the ground but instead, she kept her distance and waited patiently. When Ashlei finally turned me loose, I squared up again with Mo and waited for her attack.

"You know what, you're not even worth it. You wanna go at this shit alone, then go ahead. Fatz! We're leaving," she said.

I kept my hands up, but when Fatz came around the corner I knew that she was serious about the fight being over. The words,

"Fuck you, bitch," were on the tip of my tongue but I didn't let them fly. Beyond the blood leaking from her mouth, and behind the anger in her eyes, I saw pain. Real pain. The shit hit me a little different, and it made me act when she went to walk past me. I pulled her into my arms and held her even when she tried to pull away.

"I'm sorry, Mo. I just had to do something because I felt like I was losing my damn mind! I didn't go without you because I want to go at this shit alone...I need you by my side. I need you because I know this shit is gonna get deeper and darker, and you've gotta pull me back when I go too far."

"You don't listen, Claudette, so how can I—"

"I'll listen to you, I promise. I know you and everybody else just wants what's best for me," I said, pulling back to look at her in the eyes.

When I looked around at the people surrounding me, I could see the doubt in their eyes, but I knew they would trust me and take me at my word. When I looked back at Mo, she was giving me a look I'd seen before.

"I know if I lie, you're gonna shoot me, so you don't have to say it, Anastasia," I said.

"Good talk then. Now, where the fuck have you been? And Meatrock, I should shoot your ass for going along with her," Mo said seriously.

"You can if you want to, I'd die a happy man," he replied smiling.

"Shut your silly ass up, fool. Come on, I'll explain," I said, leading the way to the kitchen.

Everyone followed me, and once we were seated around the table, I ran down my afternoon activities. When I was done talking, all eyes swung towards Meatrock.

"What? Why are y'all staring at me?" he asked.

"Because we need to know if you laid the pipe good enough to get the job done," Ashlei said.

"Ask Snow, she could hear me putting my thing down," Meatrock replied.

Aryanna

When everyone's eyes turned towards me, I just chuckled softly while shaking my head.

"I ain't even gonna lie, he had ole girl hollering like it hurt so good. And when they came out of the room, she said she'd have what I needed sooner than later," I said.

"So, what's your play, Snow?" Ashlei asked.

"Wait and see what Nicki can find out, and then move accordingly."

All heads nodded in agreement, allowing me to breathe a sigh of relief.

"Did anyone check on our people and make sure everything was still quiet?" I asked.

"I spoke to Gunz and Vontrell not long ago, and they said shit is good at the big house," Fatz replied.

"I got a collect call from Silk, wanting to know if we'd forgotten about him," Ashlei said.

Silk was my most trusted lieutenant and probably my biggest asset in a war, but he was currently fighting a cold murder case in Virginia, which meant he was out of commission.

"That nigga knows I'd never forget him. What's it looking like out there though?" I asked.

"He didn't say much but based on his tone, I'd say he's a little more than nervous," Ashlei replied.

I contemplated her words while trying to decide what I could and should do for him.

"Mo, do either you or Ashlei have any connections to the department of corrections in Virginia?" I asked.

The quick look they exchanged spoke loudly, but I could tell there was some unease there for Mo. She looked at Fatz before speaking, but he either didn't catch the look or simply chose to ignore it.

"I-I might know someone out there, but what is it we're trying to do?" Mo asked.

"We're trying to get Silk out by any means necessary, because ain't no black man ever fared well in that racist ass state," I replied.

A Dope Boy's Queen 2

"Uh, I know he's part of your team Snow, but you're talking about pulling off a prison break while you're in the middle of a war. That don't seem smart to me," Fatz stated in a matter of fact tone.

"Are you questioning me?" I asked softly.

"That's not what he's doing, Snow, it's just—"

"He's a big boy, Anastasia, and he can speak for himself. So, are you questioning me, Fatz?" I asked again.

"No, I'm reminding you that you're working with a skeleton crew already, so you might wanna increase your body count before we're under attack, out-manned, and outgunned."

His comments were met with complete silence as all eyes locked in on me, waiting to see what my response would be to this. Part of me wanted to shoot this nigga for having the nerve to question me, but the soldier in me knew he had a very valid point.

"More people, huh? Come to think of it, I might know just the right people to handle this job in Virginia for me."

"Who, Snow?" Mo asked.

"Crazy Ashlee and her family," I replied.

The instant smile that appeared on Mo's face told me we were thinking on the same wavelength. I'd met Ashlee while she'd been in Florida on business, and her business had been disposing of a body. Her younger sister Chyna had gotten pregnant by a nothing-ass nigga, so Ashlee and her brothers Aubrey and Aaron, had decided to get rid of dude. Cutting him up into tiny pieces first had been their version of family bonding, and since making old Luke disappear, one thing I could always count on was their willingness to get more blood on their hands.

"I'll make the call and they can get Silk out, since they're closer to Virginia than us. Then we can—"

The sudden sounds of an explosion, followed closely by rapid gunfire, froze my thought in midair and had us all scrambling for our weapons. By the time I got my gun out, I could feel the ground move beneath my feet as my house shook all around us. At first, the sounds of gunfire were only coming from the front of my property, but I was suddenly hearing them in surround sound, which meant

Aryanna

whoever was attacking was doing it by land and water simultaneously.

My first instinct was to run to the basement where the weapons were stocked, and hold court from there, but we'd be fish in a barrel that way.

"Meatrock, you and I will take the front, and the rest of you take the back. The guns and ammo are downstairs."

Everyone moved without saying a word and within moments, I was creeping out of the side door to the garage with an AR-15 Diamondback clutched in my grip. I peeped around the side of the garage with the barrel of the gun, spotted a face I didn't know, and I pulled the trigger until the face I didn't know disappeared. It was early nightfall, but my front lawn was alive with sparking barrels.

At first, I thought my people were holding ground, until I heard the whine of a belt-fed machine gun, and then bodies started flying like paper in the wind. When my property was suddenly awash with a spotlight from the sky, I knew we weren't ready for the smoke they were bringing.

"Meatrock, go get everyone, we've gotta go!" I yelled over the gunfire.

He quickly disappeared as I backed up into the garage and ran to my truck. Within moments, he was back with Mo, Fatzs and Ashlei, and everybody jumped in.

"Everybody hang on," I said, starting the engine and throwing the truck into gear.

As soon as I cleared the garage, it felt like I was in a tornado because the truck was rocked on all sides by unrelenting gunfire. I kept my foot on the gas and aimed for the gate.

"Snow, that gate is reinforced steel," Mo said nervously.

"I know," I replied, willing my truck to go faster before I smacked into my target. As I got closer to the gate, I could see men, a lot of men, standing on the other side with assault rifles fastened to their waists. It looked like they were holding flame throwers though with the way those dragons were breathing fire.

I had us pointed straight for them, until the last second when I swerved, and ran straight through the gatehouse. When the body of the night worker rolled up onto my hood, I didn't even consider stopping. I just made sure to keep my foot pressed on the gas pedal. Within seconds, we were sliding sideways and shooting down the street, away from my house. I almost breathed a sigh of relief, until the street in front of us came alive with that bright ass spotlight.

Aryanna

Chapter 5

"Did Campa bring the goddamn National Guard with him?" Mo asked in disbelief.

I didn't respond, I just focused on navigating the road ahead of me. I knew nothing in the world outran a helicopter, except for a motorcycle and radio, so I was gonna have to go with plan B.

"Fatz, look in the very back and grab that RPG off of the floor," I said.

"You've got a rocket launcher in this bitch?" Ashlei asked, clearly surprised.

"Yeah. A little trick I learned from Campa, and since we can't outrun that chopper, I want you to knock that bitch out of the sky," I replied.

"No problem," Fatz said confidently.

I took a turn fast, putting my truck up on two wheels, but I managed to keep it under control and put us back on flat ground.

"Hold it steady," Fatz said, lowering the window and leaning out.

I knew he couldn't shoot that motherfucker accurately on the move, so I had my foot riding the brake in preparation.

"Stop!" he demanded.

The tires squealed in protest, and smoke blanketed us in the darkness as we slid to a stop. Seconds later, a loud scream ripped through the night, and then that beautiful big bird in the sky exploded in dramatic fashion.

"Yes!" Mo screamed excitedly.

"Fatz, call your people and tell them we're headed their way," I said, stomping on the gas again.

I didn't know if the goons Campa sent were in hot pursuit, but I wanted to put as much distance between us as possible.

"We've got a problem, Snow," Fatz said moments later.

"What now?" I asked.

"No one is answering the phone," Fatz replied.

I absorbed this information and processed it rapidly.

Aryanna

"They probably hit both houses simultaneously, but I'm betting Campa sent more firepower my way. So, we're coming in hot at the mansion, which means everybody better be ready to shoot," I said.

The sound of weapons being checked echoed through my truck loudly, and it was music to my ears. It was a short fifteen minutes later when I crept up on the mansion and stopped across from it, but from the looks of things, our guns weren't needed.

"That's a lot of cops," Ashlei said.

"Stay in the truck, I'll be back," I said, hopping out.

I looked both ways before crossing the street, looking for anybody that seemed like they didn't belong out here. My gun was legal, so I wasn't worried about walking up on the police and being armed.

"I'm sorry, ma'am, you can't be here," a cop in uniform said, holding up his hand to stop me.

"My name is Claudette Snow, and this is my house."

He looked at me skeptically, but he still grabbed his radio and called his captain. It took a few minutes for me to be let past the asshole holding down the frontline, but I quickly ran into a roadblock.

"Excuse me, ma'am, you can't—"

"This is my house," I stated, working on not showing my frustration.

"I thought this property was owned by a corporation," the cop replied.

"I own the corporation too. Given all the cops around here, do you really think I would be here if I wasn't supposed to be?"

"Well, I'll escort you to the house, but I'm not sure my captain will let you in," he said.

I motioned for him to lead the way, and I followed in his footsteps. When we made it up onto the porch, we came up on a short bald guy, commanding an audience of cops. My escort waited until they were done talking before leading me over to the man.

"Cap, this is the owner of the house."

"Mrs. Snow?" the short man asked, looking at me.

"Yes. What's going on here?"

"There was a report of gunfire, and we arrived to find a heavy firefight under way. You've got some excellent security though, because all the bodies we've found so far belong to the people who were trying to invade your house. Do you have any idea who would want to harm you?" he asked.

"No, but I just recently acquired this property a couple weeks ago. Have you identified the dead bodies?" I asked.

"Not yet, but we're working on it. I'm sorry to tell you, you can't let you go in your house right now."

Hearing these words come out of the captain's mouth froze the breath in my lungs. I was worried they'd find the mountains of coke I had hidden, but I quickly realized I was tripping.

"That's fine, Captain, just have somebody contact me whenever I can get in," I said.

"Will do, Mrs. Snow. In the meantime, I need you to come with me, and identify those who work security for you. I'd hate to let a murderer get away."

"No problem, Captain," I replied.

He led the way around the side of my property, where we came upon a group of people sitting on the cold ground of my cobblestone patio. I immediately spotted Red Gunz, Vontrell, and J5 in the mix.

"Is this everybody?" I asked.

"Yes, ma'am."

The captain thought I was talking to him, but I was actually looking at Gunz to make sure these were all our men. When he gave me a slight nod, I turned my attention towards the captain.

"These men are all under my employment, sir. Do I need to sign anything for them to be released?"

"No, Mrs. Snow, but I will have to keep the weapons my men confiscated, until after the investigation is over with."

"That's completely understandable, Captain."

He nodded his head decisively before radioing for some of his men to step around the corner and assist him with uncuffing everybody. Within a few minutes we were walking down the driveway to our respective vehicles.

"Follow me," I said to everyone.

I kept walking down the driveway, and I hopped back behind the wheel of my truck.

"What happened?" Mo asked immediately.

"I don't know, but our people are in the clear for the moment. Now we need to find somewhere to go," I said.

"Do you have any spots Campa doesn't know about?" Fatz asked.

I thought about the question, realizing I truly had no idea what Campa knew about me at this point. I knew without a doubt Phillisa would share what she knew about me, so that had to be factored in too. The enemy of your enemy was your friend, which meant they were undoubtedly working together. I started my truck and pulled off without a destination in mind. I knew there would be questions to answer whenever the cops called my house to investigate that shooting too, so I needed to get everyone settled before then.

"We're going to a hotel, and we'll figure it out from there," I said finally.

"There's no way for this many people to be inconspicuous in a hotel, Snow," Ashlei said.

"Okay, so what do you suggest, Ashlei?" I asked, with obvious frustration.

"Let's go to my house," she replied nonchalantly.

I thought that idea through, liking it more and more because I doubted Campa knew anything about Ashlei.

"You sure?" I asked, looking at her in the rearview mirror.

"I wouldn't have said it if I wasn't." I nodded and pointed my truck in the direction of her house.

There was a risk when it came to taking everyone into an environment that I was only slightly familiar with, but we still had enough artillery to protect ourselves. Forty-five minutes later, we pulled into Ashlei's driveway.

"Is there anyone in there waiting up for you, Ashlei?" I asked.

"Now bitch, you know if there was, you'd know. And they would've gotten the fuck out before we arrived," she replied, opening the back door and getting out.

A Dope Boy's Queen 2

We all followed her lead out into the crisp night air, and on into her house. Despite having no kids and no man, Ashlei had a big house with five bedrooms. I'd asked her before why she needed so much damn space, and she'd told me being in the projects all her life pushed her to be that way. I could definitely understand and relate to that, so I never questioned her again. Right now, I was glad she'd felt the need for all this space.

"Gunz, lead everyone to the basement," I said, holding the front door open for everyone to come through.

I let them go to the basement, while I went to the kitchen in search of something to drink. Thankfully, I found an unopened bottle of Bacardi 151 on the counter, and I moved towards it like gravity was pulling me.

"Take it easy, Snow," Ashlei said, coming into the kitchen.

I ignored her words and kept the bottle tipped to my lips, trying to drain the contents in one gulp. The burning alcohol had my eyes watering, but I pushed through and kept drinking.

"Snow, come on," Ashlei said, putting her hand on my shoulder.

I shook her off and took two more huge swallows, before lowering the bottle to catch my breath.

"Do you feel better now?" she asked sarcastically.

"A little, yeah. I'm just getting started though."

"Do you really think that's what you need to do? I mean damn, bitch, you're no good to us drunk as fuck," she said, snatching the bottle from my grip.

Before I could reach to grab it back, she raised it high over her head, and brought it crashing down to the floor forcefully. The bottle shattered instantly, sending pieces of flying glass in every direction.

"Snow!" Mo yelled, running into the room with her gun up and at the ready.

"I'm fine," I said, raising my hand and waving it so she'd put her gun away.

Fatz came barreling into the room quickly behind Mo, but he pulled short when he saw us just standing there. He took one look at what was left of the gallon bottle, and backed out of the room quietly.

"What happened?" Mo asked, looking at me closely.

"Nothing. Ashlei was giving me some good advice," I replied, looking at Ashlei and winking.

"It was a necessary conversation to have. We're counting on you to lead us out of this darkness, Snow, so we need you to be on top of your game like never before," Ashlei said genuinely.

"I got you," I replied.

"So, what's the plan, Snow?" Mo asked.

"I haven't gotten that far yet, but for now, I want everyone to hold up here. It might be the only safe place we have left. I'm going down to the police station, so they don't come looking for me to ask questions."

"What are you gonna tell them?" Mo asked.

"That as a top-notch attorney, I've surely made my fair share of enemies. It could be a victim's family who feels like I shouldn't have gotten an accused murderer off. It could be a client who feels like I should've gotten them less time, or even their family for that matter."

"So, you're gonna throw them off the trail of what's really going on?" Mo said.

"A war hurts business. Campa knows that, so I'm thinking he's trying to kill two birds with one stone. I'll handle the legal angle officially. And unofficially, I'll talk to my people on the payroll, so they know what's really going on. After that is taken care of, I can figure out how to kill this motherfucker," I said through clenched teeth.

The thought of both Campa and Phillisa kneeling before me with my gun pressed to their heads, made my pussy throb. I wanted these slippery motherfuckers in the worst way!

"While you're gone, we'll put our collective heads together, and try to figure out how best to help you," Mo said.

"And I'll go to the storage unit to grab some weapons," Ashlei offered.

"Get all of the weapons, Ash, and take some cars that no one would recognize. Matter of fact, take Vontrell and a few of his men with you," I said.

She nodded her understanding, and she and Mo left the room. I used the rare moment to myself to think through the next few hours. I knew there would be a lot of questions from the cops, but I was a seasoned lawyer, so I wouldn't be rattled. While I went over the predictable line of questioning in my mind, I got a broom and dustpan out of Ashlei's pantry and cleaned up the liquor bottle.

When that was done, I made my way to the basement to touch bases with Gunz and J5. No one wanted me to leave the house by myself, and once I saw the logical argument I was making wasn't gaining traction, I agreed to Mo going with me. Fatz had volunteered, but he looked like a hitta, and that wasn't what you walked into a police station with. After our little meeting of the minds concluded, Mo and I went out to my truck and left.

"He came harder than I expected," Mo said.

"Yeah, he did. He's determined, but so am I!"

"Did you ever envision this day coming?" she asked.

"No. At least not until after he killed Tony right in front of me. He took something from me that day, and I didn't think he understood that at the time, but I'm betting that's when he started planning."

"I remember how distraught you were that night. I'd never seen you like that... Well, at least not since Zion..."

She let her sentence trail off, and I was sure that our thoughts were traveling in the same direction. At the time I'd felt like losing my husband, the love of my life, was the worst pain ever. But the pain of his betrayal was like a thousand tiny cuts to my heart, and I still didn't know how to heal from that.

"He still loved you, Snow. I know that may be hard to believe, but I know he still loved you."

I looked over at her to see if she was serious, and I didn't see the hint of a smile anywhere on her face.

"And you figure this how?" I asked, turning my eyes back on the road.

Aryanna

"Because a side bitch never compares to the queen, or she ceases to be a side bitch. Zion never gave that bitch a title or anything more than some sweat that quickly dried on her skin. Now, that don't excuse a damn thing, but it should put it into perspective a little."

I gave her words careful consideration, instead of dismissing them out of hand like I wanted to. I could admit she might be speaking some truth, but at this point it didn't matter. My nigga sticking his dick in another bitch had changed everybody's lives forever, and he wasn't here to suffer the consequences. He'd made sure that I had to go through this alone. Thankfully, I had a strong support system to light my way in the darkness. They thought I was their light, but the love of the people around me continued to save me.

"I love you, Anastasia Morano."

"I know, bitch, and I love you too," she replied, reaching over and taking my hand.

Her touch was comforting and I held onto her, knowing I would face many a day when I needed her. I considered myself to be as ruthless as they came, and as a woman in the streets, I had to be just that. But this situation had exposed my vulnerability, and I didn't like it. I didn't like it one goddamn bit! I wasn't used to my pain impacting my decisions in the streets, and for it to happen now made me question myself in an unfamiliar way. I knew second-guessing could lead to imminent death, and I was trying to avoid that for mine and my son's sake.

"I need to call and check on Junior," I said, pulling my hand apart from hers, and grabbing my phone.

"I'm sure he's fine, and still enjoying his time with Alexia."

"Yeah, well, your stepdaughter better not corrupt my baby boy," I warned, dialing Zion Junior's cellphone number.

Before the phone could ring in my ear, my phone started vibrating in my hand. I looked to see who was calling me, but I didn't recognize the number.

"Who is this?" I asked, answering the call.

"It's Ashlee."

A Dope Boy's Queen 2

"Whose phone are you calling me from, and why didn't you use your phone?" I asked, confused.

"Because we've got a problem, and I don't trust my phone," she replied.

"Problem, what problem?"

I listened intently as she spoke and when she was done speaking, I hung up.

"What is it, Snow?" Mo asked.

"It-It's Silk and Jeezy… They're dead."

Aryanna

Chapter 6

"Wait, what?" Mo asked, shocked.

"Ashlee just called and said her people in Virginia contacted her and said Silk was found damn near decapitated. They've got some hitta named Marc under arrest for it, but it's all circumstantial. And Jeezy... they found Jeezy floating in the Hudson River in pieces."

Her silence after I gave her the update I'd just received, spoke for both of us. Two niggas in my crew I considered la familia, were made examples of and in my heart, I knew it was my fault. No one besides Campa could've gotten to my dudes, and he's just proved that no one was safe.

"I-I don't understand how someone could get to either of them. I mean, Jeezy was in New York with his homies, and Silk was locked the fuck up!" Mo said, in a voice still laced with disbelief.

"This was his plan all along. The case against Silk was bullshit, and he'd said as much. And Jeezy, I knew it was weird as fuck for him to be summoned home all of a sudden. Campa has been lining this up, and I never saw it fucking coming. I suspected he'd been behind the unexplained attempts on my life, but I've got no doubt now."

"So, what do we do now?" she asked.

I let that question hang between us until I'd pulled up into the parking lot of the police station.

"Do you trust me, Mo?" I asked, turning in my seat to face her.

"You know I do, so don't ask me no dumb shit."

"Okay, I just need you to keep trusting me. I'll get us out of this, and we'll come out on top, I can promise you that. Now, I'm about to go in here and sell this story of me not knowing shit to these nice police. While I'm doing that, I want you to reach out to Ashlee in Tennessee and tell her I need her and her family out here, ASAP. Pay for their travel and put them in one of my vacant properties. I'll handle the rest," I said, opening my door and stepping out.

"I got you, Snow."

Aryanna

Experience had taught me that at a time like this, most people would panic or be in such emotional upheaval, that they were too distracted to put up an adequate defense. I was opposite though because this situation was giving me laser focus. I now understood what I had to do, and it was simple. I had to not give a fuck and kill anybody standing between me and my goal.

As I walked up the front walk towards the police station, I was texting Nicki, telling her I needed results on my investment immediately. I narrowed her focus to Campa, only because I knew all things had to be going through him. Phillisa was still a worthy adversary, but it was Campa who was coming for me. They were definitely a two-headed monster, so I had to take it one head at a time.

It was three hours later when I walked back out of the police station and climbed back behind the wheel of my truck.

"I thought you would've got some sleep while I was gone, I said, looking at Mo's wide eyes.

"Nope, I've been working. Do you wanna know what I've accomplished?"

"Sure," I replied, yawning as I started my truck and pulled off.

"Well, Ashlee is on the way here, and she's bringing company. Her sisters, Lexx and Chyna are coming, as well as her brothers, Aubrey and Aaron. All I had to tell her was that you were in trouble, and she said they'd be here by dawn."

Hearing this made me smile, because there was nothing I loved more than loyalty.

"Once I was done with that call, I woke up the Lamborghini dealer I know, and bought three identical black 2023 Gallardo's, completely bulletproof for everything except large explosives. I had to use an extra million of your money to have them ready by lunch tomorrow. From now on, we move as a very fast motorcade. I also bought a half dozen 2020 Ducati motorcycles so we can put shooters around our cars."

"Am I to assume the Lambo's are for you, me, and Ashlei?" I asked, looking over at her.

"Of course. I mean, shit, we're getting shot at as much as you are."

"You've got a point there," I conceded.

"Thank you. When I was done with transportation, I hit up our weapons people and ordered enough shit to invade Syria twice in the same year. I didn't know where you wanted it delivered, so as soon as you tell me that, I'll get back on it. Lastly, when you came out, I was working on buying a couple different properties. A warehouse, and two houses in the Keys to be exact."

"What name are you getting them under?" I asked warily.

"I'm using my name, because I doubt either Campa or Phillisa thinks to look for me. I didn't wanna use your name, or the name of the corporation you used to snatch Campa's house."

"Good girl," I said, smiling at her.

"I try. I'd love to tell you this fixes all of our problems, but I still haven't had any luck tracking these motherfuckers," she said, shaking her head in frustration.

"It's okay. They can only hide for so long, and I'll be there when they poke their heads out."

"We'll be there with you," she vowed.

"I know, and I'm hoping that moment comes sooner than later. That little session I just had with our people helped too."

"What do you mean? I thought you were meeting with the police about the two shootings?" she asked, confused.

"Oh, I took care of that first, and then I slid off into a back room to have a little chat with the people I pay handsomely to do the legal dirty work. As of an hour ago, the eyes of the law were looking for Phillisa and Campa. Not just in Florida either, I've got eyes everywhere looking for them, with specific instructions that I want then alive."

"How high up did you run that request?" she asked.

"I told the locals to reach out to their counterparts in both the FBI and CIA."

I could see her nodding her head, signaling that she liked what I was doing.

"I've already got my ears to the streets from the inside," she said.

"Is Ashlei on the same page with you?"

Aryanna

"Of course. We're both gonna be working alternating schedules, so that one of us is always by your side," she replied.

"I need a list of new hittas too, but make sure you vet them thoroughly. The last thing I want is to have a Trojan horse situation, and we let the enemy in through the front door," I said.

"Understood. Where do you want the weapons sent?"

I thought about this carefully, knowing that these weapons were more than essential with the way we were being attacked.

"Put them in the new warehouse you're trying to buy. If that deal falls through for some reason, then let me know, and we'll go from there," I replied.

"I'll make sure it goes through."

I liked to hear that determination in her voice. The sudden ringing of my phone got our attention, and since I trusted her more than anyone else, I answered it through the truck's Bluetooth.

"Yeah?"

"Snow, it's Nicki. They're in Cuba."

"Good work, Nicki. I'll come to your spot so you can give me the details," I replied.

"Or you could send Antonio," Nicki said quickly.

"Antonio? Meatrock actually told you his real name?" Mo asked in disbelief.

"I guess you two really hit it off," I said, chuckling softly.

"Uh, yeah we did, so…"

"So, I'll send him right away," I said, shaking my head.

"Thanks. I'll have him back by mid-morning."

"Wait, mid—"

My question was cut off by the fact that she'd hung up the phone, and I had no doubt it was on purpose.

"Damn, the dick must have been good as fuck!" Mo said laughing.

I couldn't help laughing with her because this shit was crazy. At this point, I couldn't figure out if I was a queen pin or a pimp. I just knew I had to do whatever to keep us all alive. Before I could discuss the possibility of what moves we'd have to make in Cuba, my phone rang again. I answered immediately, thinking that it was Nicki again.

"You change your mind already, bitch, or do you want more than one of my niggas this time?" I asked.

"Hello, Claudette."

The sound of her voice forced me to hit the brakes and bring the truck to a screeching halt in the middle of the road. I could hear other car tires screeching as horns blared, but I wasn't focused on any of that. I looked over at Mo to see if I was losing my damn mind, but the look on her face told me we'd both heard the same thing.

"I-I know goddamn well you didn't have the balls to call me," I growled through clenched teeth.

"Not balls, just pussy. Good pussy. I was hoping you'd listen to me, and I knew seeing you face-to-face would only entice you to kill me."

"Oh bitch, I'm gonna kill you no matter what, and that's a promise!" I yelled, getting angrier by the second.

I felt Mo's hand on my arm, forcing me to look at her, and I saw her mouth the words, "Keep her talking." She was pulling out her phone and texting someone rapidly, and I knew it was most likely one of our tech people. It hurt beyond the physical to think about staying on the phone with this bitch, but I knew it was for the greater good.

"I'm listening, bitch," I said reluctantly.

"I'm sure you are, just like I'm sure you're trying to trace this call. It's a waste of time but knock yourself out. The reason I'm calling is to make it clear to you that I'm in no way involved in the attack against you and your people. I don't wanna hurt you in any way."

"It's a little late for that, don't you think?" I asked sarcastically.

"Claudette, I-I truly never meant to hurt you. My love for Zion was—"

"Don't!" I growled, squeezing the steering wheel so tight that my hands hurt.

Aryanna

"I can't justify what happened with Zion, and I'm not trying to…I can't regret it either though, just like I don't regret any moment you and I shared."

My eyes quickly cut to Mo's face as I felt myself blush, and the hurt I saw she couldn't hide made me madder.

"We never shared a moment, you grimy hoe, we fucked and that was it," I stated heatedly.

The effortless sound of her laugh floated through my truck, making it feel like she was in the seat beside me. That shit took my anger to the next level, and before I could stop myself, I hung up on her ignorant ass. I was breathing so hard I felt like I would start foaming at the mouth any minute. The sound of impatient horns made me push the gas pedal to the floor, and speed away in a cloud of smoke.

"I'm gonna murder that bitch!" I vowed passionately.

"Not if I get to her trifling ass first," Mo said sincerely.

When my phone started ringing again, I was about to answer it from the handset, but Mo hit the button to engage the Bluetooth first.

"Listen bitch, if you ain't got something productive to say, then save your breath for sucking dick."

"It's nice to hear your voice, Mo. I bet you're loving this shit, ain't you?" Phillisa asked confidently.

This time it was Mo's laughter that came fast and effortless and when I looked at her, I could see through the shadows that it was genuine.

"Snow could never love a bitch like you, and do you know why? Because you're transparent and fake as fuck. You're good for some fun, but before the cum dries on your face, her attention was back on the real people in her life," Mo replied.

"You sure about that, Morano? Because if you were confident in your words then you wouldn't have felt as threatened as you did before shit went sideways. You can lie to yourself all you want, but if you really wanna know the truth, just look Claudette in the eyes. I promise you'll see more than lust."

"Fuck that dumb shit you talking, because it's irrelevant. Whenever I see you, wherever I see you, you're dead," I vowed.

My declaration left her quiet for a few seconds, but I knew that wouldn't last.

"Snow, I don't wanna kill you…that wouldn't be fair to Junior or—"

"If you ever mention my son again, I'll kill you in the most gruesome way that I can think of," I said softly, projecting nothing but cold fury into my voice.

"Claudette…please," Phillisa said.

"Save your please for the day we meet," Mo said, hanging up again.

I didn't say anything, nor did I give a fuck whether or not she called back. I just kept driving, trying to stop my skin from crawling from the sound of her voice still ringing in my ears. It took about fifteen minutes to pull up in front of Ashlei's house, but after I turned the engine off, neither of us moved.

"She's trying to get in your ear," Mo said finally.

"I know. Yours too."

That shit ain't gonna work," she replied.

"You sure?"

I looked over at her when I asked the question, but she didn't immediately turn to face me. That was an answer in itself.

"What do you wanna ask me, Mo?"

"Did you love her?"

"I don't know," I replied honestly.

"You barely knew her, Claudette!"

"No one can control love, Anastasia, and it doesn't come with a timetable. So, I don't know if I loved her. But I know I don't now. Which is more important to you?"

When she turned to look at me, I could see the frustration and pain clearly through the moonlight bathing my truck. I'd never known before this moment how much my involvement with Phillisa had hurt Mo, and now I could never forget the look she was giving me.

"Can I ask you something, Mo?"

Aryanna

"What?"

"Are you in love with me?" I asked seriously.

"For you to have to ask that question means you ain't been paying attention to shit, bitch, but I'll answer your question anyway...I'm not gay, and to be honest, I never really fucked with women until you. I've kissed them before and fooled around, but there's never been anything to the extent of you and me. I still don't consider myself gay...maybe bisexual or bi-curious. At the end of the day, it's you though. It's my unconditional love for you that brings my mind and body alive. So, to answer your question, yeah, I'm in love with you, but it's deeper than that."

"Believe it or not, I actually understand that. I love you in a way no one else, male or female, can touch. So, it doesn't matter what I felt for Phillisa, or even how much I loved Zion, because what's between you and I is above all of that. I need you to understand that shit, and I mean understand it in both your heart and mind. Don't let anyone come between us, Anastasia, you hear me?"

"I hear you," she replied, taking my hand in hers.

I pulled her towards me and kissed her gently. The feeling of her hand on the back of my neck and pulling me closer, had me trying to climb into the passenger seat.

"We-we should take this in the house," I said in between kisses.

"Mmm-hmm...God, if you had a dick, I'd let you get me pregnant," she said, laughing as she pulled away from me.

For a moment I just stared at her as my mind raced faster than any bullet I'd ever fired.

"Are you okay, Claudette? You're looking at me with crazy eyes."

"That's because you're a goddamn genius, bitch," I said softly.

"Huh?"

"On the phone, Phillisa said she wasn't trying to justify her relationship with Zion, but she couldn't regret it either...Do you know why she has no regrets?" I asked.

"Uh no, but I'm assuming you somehow do now."

"I do, and I should've seen it sooner," I replied, shaking my head in frustration.

"Okay, well enlighten me, because you just fucked up the whole mood with this epiphany."

"She has no regrets because of her son. The son she had by Zion."

Aryanna

Chapter 7

"Phillisa has a son...and you think it's Zion's?" Mo asked slowly.
"Yes."
"How old is her son, and where is he?" she asked.
"I don't know how old he is, but he's in Columbia, I think."
"Well, if you don't know how old he is how do you know he's Zion's? Have you seen him, or a picture of him?" she asked.
"No, I haven't seen him or a picture of him. Shit, I don't even know his name, but I've got a gut feeling about this," I replied smiling.
"I don't know, Claudette, I think your reaching."
"Maybe, but if I'm right, then I'm about to change the game," I said, opening my door and hopping out of the truck.
"Whoa, hold up, change the game how?"
I didn't respond to her question, but I heard her coming behind me. I opened the door to Ashlei's house, calling her name as I went. I could hear Mo coming behind me, but I didn't stop to wait for her. I went straight to Ashlei's room and opened the door without knocking.
"Wake up, bitch!" I hollered.
The way she hopped out of bed wide-eyed, while grabbing her gun off the nightstand, told me she'd been sleeping real light.
"Put the gun down, it's just me," I said.
"What-what's wrong? Are you hurt?"
"Nah, just come out to the kitchen," I said, turning and walking back out of the room.
I almost ran over Mo on the way, but I grabbed her by the arm and pulled her along with me.
"What the hell do you mean you're about to change the game, Claudette?"
"Patience, my dear Anastasia," I replied.
"Stop using my first name, dammit!" I laughed at this request, but I didn't say it again.
I sat down at the kitchen table while pushing Mo into the seat next to me. A few moments later, Ashlei joined us by taking the seat

across from me. I could tell by the way she was fighting not to yawn that I needed to get straight to the point, because her attention was still on her sheets.

"Okay, so I think Phillisa's son is Zion's son, and I wanna kidnap him," I said.

I couldn't tell if it was the nonchalant delivery that I used to deliver this news, or the content of the news itself, but both women were staring at me with wide eyes and slack jaws.

"Phillisa had a baby by Zion for real? "And you wanna kidnap him?" Mo asked slowly.

"Yes, and yes," I replied.

"Wait, when the fuck did she have Zion's baby?" Ashlei asked.

"She's not completely sure, because she doesn't know how old the little boy is, or if he's Zion's son for real," Mo said.

"And you wanna kidnap him?" I said.

"Yep," I replied.

The two of them exchanged a look that was easy to interpret.

"I'm not crazy, so you two can miss me with that shit. I know in my gut Phillisa's son was fathered by Zion, because it's the only thing that makes sense. If I'm wrong though, we still can't lose by snatching him up and forcing her to come to us," I said.

They exchanged a look again, but I knew this one was to see who would speak first.

"Okay, so let's say you're right, Snow. How are we supposed to get to him? You said he's in Columbia, and I'm certain Phillisa would have security around him," Mo said.

"Undoubtedly, she does, but I doubt I'm perceived as an enemy to her people back home. I mean after all, she did just bring me to the table with all the major players, which means she'd have to explain how and why shit went left. Her admitting to fucking her new partner's husband, and explaining the fallout behind it, could get her killed. So, for that reason alone, I feel comfortable going to Columbia and picking up her son without having to fire a shot," I concluded.

"But Snow, she's probably in Columbia by now, so—"

"No, she's in Cuba with her father," Mo said, staring at me closely.

"When did we find that out?" Ashlei asked, looking back and forth between Mo and me.

"When she called Snow about thirty minutes ago," Mo replied.

"That bitch actually had the nerve to call you?" Ashlei asked in disbelief.

"Yeah, and now I'm glad she did because she gave me what I needed to bring her to her knees," I said, smiling genuinely.

"Okay, so what's the plan, Snow?" Ashlei asked.

"I'm still working on that, so we'll reconvene after I get some sleep," I replied, standing up and stretching mightily.

I could tell I had their attention and they wanted to discuss this more, but there was really no point in it.

"Where are you sleeping?" Mo asked.

"In Ashlei's room. You and Fatz take the guest room," I replied.

"Fatz is already in there snoring and shit," Ashlei said, shaking her head.

"I'll see you two in the morning," I said, heading towards Ashlei's room.

When I rounded the corner, I could hear them start talking again, but that was okay because I knew they were trying to formulate a back-up plan to whatever my plan would be. That was how great teams functioned, they had to anticipate what I wouldn't see.

When I got back to Ashlei's room, I didn't bother stripping my clothes off. I put my gun on the nightstand closest to me, kicked my shoes off, and attacked her sheets like we had issues that talking couldn't resolve. It felt like I was asleep within seconds, and I welcomed the slumber like a kid would ice cream in the summertime. My sleep was dreamless, until I heard a familiar voice pierce my inner sanctum.

"I didn't come all this way to watch your silly ass sleep, bitch."

I cracked one eye open to find Ashlee sitting on the bed beside me. I hadn't seen her beautiful face framed by her long blonde hair in a long time, but the relief I felt at her presence was a feeling I remembered. I knew this bitch had my back come hell or high water.

Aryanna

"Ain't nobody tell you to be watching me sleep, weirdo," I replied, smiling up at her.

She smiled back at me before hugging me fiercely.

"You're just lucky I didn't wake your ass up sooner, bitch, because waiting ain't never been my thing."

"What time is it?" I asked, noticing how bright it was in Ashlei's bedroom.

"Damn near noon! No wonder you can't hunt a motherfucker down, you're too busy getting beauty rest."

"Fuck you, bitch, I've been running nonstop!" I replied laughing.

"Yeah, that's what your home girl said. By the way, that Spanish bitch is bad!"

"No, Ashlee," I said, pushing her off me so I could get up.

"No, what?"

"I know you, bitch, and you're a pussy hound!" I said, laughing as I got up and grabbed my pistol off the nightstand.

"Well yeah, but that's not a bad thing."

"Business before pleasure, Ash, now come on," I said, pulling her up off the bed.

I led the way out of the room and followed the smell of food into the kitchen.

"Well damn, I hope one of you hungry motherfuckers thought to save me some," I said.

All eyes turned on me, but I didn't feel any nervousness. When Aubrey cracked a smile and hurried to scoop me off my feet, I couldn't do anything except giggle like a schoolgirl. I couldn't put into words how happy I was that my extended family had kept their promise and showed up with everyone in tow. Once Aubrey had squeezed me enough, he put me down, and Aaron picked me right up. Aubrey and Aaron were brothers for sure, but one might not know that simply by looking at them.

Aubrey had sandy blond hair and blue eyes, but Aaron had brown hair and brown eyes. Aaron was the bigger of the two, but just barely with his six foot one, two-hundred-thirty-pound frame. Aubrey's six-foot, one hundred-seventy-pound frame could be very misleading though, because his hands were lightning quick and just as accurate as his brother's. Boxing was how they kept their shit quick. Putting the two of them together meant a guaranteed ass whooping for several people.

"Your muscles are cutting me," I said, laughing.

"That's just his bony chest," Alexas said, chuckling.

"That's a lie, and you know it," Aaron said, putting me back on my feet.

I turned to face Ashlee's two little sisters, who were standing behind Aaron. The boys in the family might've had different characteristics, but the beauty of the women made their relation undeniable. Alexas and Chyna had the same dirty blonde hair as Ashlee did, but all of them wore it at different lengths.

Lexx was five foot eleven, with one hundred sixty pounds of curves to match her beautiful face, but Chyna doll was only five foot two, with one hundred and thirty pounds that gave her body a lean gracefulness. Their beauty fooled everyone though, because they were some mean bitches, and they were with all the shit.

"Get over here," I said, opening my arms wide so Lexx and Chyna could hug me.

We spent a few moments doing the girl thing by trying to talk over each other and catch up on everything we'd missed in each other's lives.

"I can't believe you two bitches had kids without me being there," I said, looking at Alexas and Chyna with a genuine hurt expression.

"Lexx had two, I only had one," Chyna said.

"We should've told you, but in our defense, you've obviously been busy," Lexx replied.

I had to acknowledge the truth in what she was saying and move away from the hurt I felt.

"When this is over, I'm coming to Tennessee to see my godchildren," I informed both women.

"You better," Chyna said,

"So, let's get down to business!" Aubrey said, breaking up our reunion by handing me a plate of food.

I took the plate and went to the table to sit down.

"How much did Mo tell you?" I asked.

"I gave them the highlights, but they need the whole breakdown," Mo said from her position across the table from me.

I nodded my head and started eating, while trying to figure out where to start this crazy story. Since I knew everyone in the kitchen was family bound by loyalty, I decided to omit nothing. Once I started talking, the whole sordid tale spilled out rapidly, and I had to use bites of food to take a breath. When I was done talking, all eyes rested on me, but I could tell Ashlee and her siblings were thinking swiftly. I gave them all the time they needed to process while I got up and took my empty plate to the sink.

"I'm going to Columbia with you," Ashlee said from behind me.

"If you're going, then we're all going," Aubrey said quickly.

I turned around to find him staring at his sister with a determined look on his face that was easy to interpret.

"Don't you two start. We've gotta split up into teams, because we're fighting more than one opponent," I said.

"So, you don't believe the shit Phillisa told you?" Ashlei asked.

"Fuck no! That bitch is in this with dear old dad, but even if she ain't, she's still gotta answer for all that she's done," I replied.

"What's the first move?" Aaron asked.

"We go to Columbia. I'm taking a team of women with me, because we'll appear nonthreatening that way. Mo, Ashlee, and Lexx will go with me. Ashlei, I need you here because you need to go to work, and handle shit around here. Mo, I want you to get with her about all the moves you made while I was at the police station last night.

"Aubrey, Aaron, and Fatz, I want you all to hold the fort down. I want you to take delivery of the new weapons and secure the new properties so they can withstand an invasion. All of my men will be at your disposal because I can't show up in Columbia pretending to be a friend with an army. Any questions?" I asked.

When nobody replied, I nodded and smiled.

"Snow, we need to go get these cars and bikes," Mo said.

"Bikes?" Aubrey inquired, smiling at me.
"Figures you'd lock in on that word," I said chuckling.
"You know how I get down," he replied.
"I do, so you should come with us," I suggested amicably.

He agreed without hesitation, and once I told Ashlei and Mo they had to come so they could drive back, we prepared to leave. Before I could walk out of the kitchen, Fatz grabbed me by the arm and pulled me close, so he could whisper in my ear.

"You make sure you all come back in one piece. If shit feels off in any way, you shoot first."

"I'll bring her back to you," I replied in the same low tone.

I knew that he knew I was block tested and hood approved, so what he was really saying was, I better not get Mo killed. I didn't take offense because we both loved her, and I understood the liability that made us.

"It's not just about her, Snow...I care about you too," he said seriously.

His words warmed me in a way that was foreign, but it still felt good. I kissed him on his cheek quickly, and then walked from the room. I went out to my truck and waited for everyone to follow me out. I sent a text to my people watching both ends of the street Ashlei lived on and told them we'd be on the move momentarily. Five minutes later, we were on the road to the Lamborghini dealership in downtown Miami. It took less than an hour for me to sign all the paperwork necessary for us to drive away with the three brand-new black bulletproof beauties.

From that dealership, we went up the block to the Ducati dealer so that I could tell him where to deliver my bikes. Aubrey picked out the one she wanted, and then we were back on the move. I had one of my men drive my truck because I wanted to get a feel for the Lambo, and that bitch felt great! It was like riding on a cloud. A really fast cloud!

Once we got back to Ashlei's house, I made all the necessary arrangements for our travel to Columbia. The only way to go was to fly private, which meant I was giving advanced warning to the cartel of my arrival. To say that I wasn't nervous would've been a lie, but I put the nerves to the side for the sake of something bigger. Within an hour Ashlee, Mo, Chyna, and Alexas and I were boarding the G3 I'd chartered.

"Alright, so how is this gonna go once we're on the ground?" Ashlee asked.

"Well, I'm sending word through the dark net that I'm coming to town with some friends to pick up Phillisa's son," I replied.

"And you think it's gonna be that easy?" Lexx asked.

"Yes, and I'll tell you why. These ain't the type of people you fuck with, so it's one of those situations where you wouldn't be there unless you were supposed to be there. Nobody would stick their head in the lion's mouth," I said.

"Nobody except your crazy ass," Mo said, shaking her head.

It was pointless to argue against what she was saying, considering that we were taxiing down the runway for takeoff. Once we were in the air, I sent the message to Phillisa's uncle that I was en route and set to rendezvous with Phillisa once she finished up her latest business deal. I knew by telling him that she was busy without blatantly saying it, would prevent him from calling her. He was old school, so he knew the hazards of being distracted while dealing with life and death situations. It took him about twenty minutes to hit me back, but when he did, I breathed a sigh of relief.

"It's on," I said, locking eyes with Mo.

"So, we're just supposed to breeze into town, pick up the kid, and disappear into thin air?" Chyna asked.

I could see the skepticism in the wrinkles on her unblemished forehead.

"Let me break it down for you all. Phillisa's people already knew we were at war with Campa, so the recent bloodshed won't be a surprise to them. Neither will the notion that Phillisa would want to protect her son herself, so she'd send someone she trusts to pick him up. That would be me. Furthermore, they would know Campa wouldn't know about his grandson's existence, but if he did know that, then he would be in danger. All the more reason for a mother to be overprotective," I concluded.

"You're an evil genius, bitch," Lexx said, shaking her head.

A Dope Boy's Queen 2

I could tell everyone understood why this would work, but the look in Morano's eyes told me she still didn't like the play I was making. I didn't question her loyalty, I just wished we were on the same page. We all spent the flight going over details of the escape plan should shit get sticky, and by the time we landed, everyone knew their position to play.

When we filed down the steps of the plane, I was looking for the trademark SUV's that would take us to wherever Phillisa's son was but instead, there was only one truck waiting. The back door opened when I stepped to the forefront, and I saw a familiar face. When I been brought out here the first time I'd had to go through an inquisition, and the man walking towards me had been a part of that.

"It's good to see you again, Mrs. Snow. I figured that I would save us time and get you on your way by bringing little Asad to you," he said.

"I appreciate that...Where is Asad?" I asked.

With a glance over his shoulder, the other back door of the black Range Rover opened, and a small figure appeared. Without hesitation, he came to stand beside the man, and when I got a look at his face my heart stopped.

"Holy shit," Lexx mumbled.

"Asad, these are the friends of your mom's that I told you about. I want you to go with them and behave yourself."

"So," Asad replied quietly.

He hugged the man before making his way over to me. He stopped in front of me and stared up into my face. I opened my mouth to speak, but suddenly the world waved in front of me and blackness surrounded me.

Aryanna

Chapter 8

I felt like I was floating through the darkness, but I felt a peacefulness that only came from my baby boy's smile. I could feel myself wanting to look for Junior, but before I could, I caught the whiff of a horrible smell that made me want to vomit.

"Wh-what the fuck!" I exclaimed, fighting the rolling in my stomach as I opened my eyes.

My vision was blurry for a few moments, and then I saw Mo leaning over me with something clasped in her hand.

"Are you okay?" she asked.

"What the fuck is that smell?" I asked.

"Smelling salts," she replied, waving a small vial in her hand.

"Y-you put that shit up to my nose? Bitch, are you crazy?" I growled.

"You passed out, Snow, calm down," Ashlee said.

I looked to my left where I found her sitting comfortably in the leather of the plane's chair, preparing to dispute the bullshit she was saying. I just barely got my mouth open when my eyes skated past her to the little boy sitting on the leather couch beside her. The feeling of wanting to throw up came back with a vengeance, but for a different reason.

"He looks just like Junior," I whispered.

"I know," Mo said, taking my hand in hers.

I turned my eyes back towards the ceiling of the plane and let the silent tears clouding my vision swim towards my ears. I hadn't realized the pain that would hit me if my epiphany proved to be true, but I understood now. I could feel what was left of my heart shattering in my chest, and there was no way to stop it. I didn't need to ask the little boy a single question to know he was Zion's son, but I knew there would have to be some type of conversation between us.

Closing my eyes allowed me to gather my strength and mental fortitude for all that would come next. When I opened them again, I'd managed to turn down the volume of the screaming going on in my mind. I really wished I could turn it off completely, but that was impossible.

Aryanna

"Where are we?" I asked Mo.

"Headed home. We've been in the air for about two hours," she replied.

"How did you explain me passing out?"

"Exhaustion," she said simply.

I nodded my head in appreciation, while struggling to sit up on the couch I was occupying.

Mo backed up to give me room as I swung my legs to the floor. I could feel little Asad's eyes on me before I even met his gaze, but when I looked him directly in the eyes, I didn't see the worry I'd anticipated. There was only open curiosity. I patted the space next to me, and he only showed a moment's hesitation before getting up and coming beside me.

"How old are you, Asad?" I asked.

"I'm six. Why?"

"You're big for your age," I replied, dodging his question.

"My mom tells me that a lot."

"What else does she tell you?" I asked.

"That I look like my daddy," he said, smiling proudly.

"You do," I mumbled.

I could feel Mo staring at me, but I kept my attention on Asad.

"Where is your dad?" I asked.

"In heaven. My mom said that he had to go there when I was still little, but it's okay, because he still loves me."

There was a part of me that wanted to be furious with this little boy for talking about my husband, but the reality was that he was as innocent as me in this situation. He wasn't wrong for loving Zion, any more than I was. Knowing this didn't make my heart hurt less, it simply controlled the part of my brain that was tempted to rip his world apart with some harsh truth.

"Listen Asad, your mom is off handling some very important business, so you're gonna stay with me for a little while," I said.

"Where do you stay, and when will I get to see my mom?"

His questions told me just how smart he was, but that didn't worry me.

"I stay in the United States. Florida to be more exact."

"My mom goes to Florida a lot, and she always brings me something back when she comes home," he said, smiling that same smile that I'd seen on my own son's face countless times before.

I was struggling to breathe normally, and it felt like I was on the verge of having some type of panic attack, but I fought through it.

"Well, now you get to see the land where she spends so much time," I said, forcing a smile on my face.

"Okay, but can we get something to eat first?"

His request drew snickers from everyone.

"Come on, honey, I'm sure we can find something on this big plane for you to snack on," Lexx said, rising from her seat and holding out her hand to him.

Asad got up without hesitation and went with her, which gave Mo room to take his seat.

"Are you okay, sweetheart?" she asked, gently.

I looked at her, knowing she could see right to my soul where the true answer to that question resided.

"He looks just like Junior," I said for the second time.

"Yeah, there's no denying that. I was hoping you weren't right before we made this journey, because I didn't wanna see the look on your face that I'm seeing right now."

"He-he was really fucking that bitch…and he had a baby with her," I said, trying not to cry any more tears.

"That still doesn't mean he loved her on the level he did you, so—"

"Doesn't it though, Anastasia? I mean, he could've made her have an abortion, if for no other reason than to keep his family intact. He didn't do that though, did he?" I asked rhetorically.

"You don't believe in abortion, Claudette, so what makes you think Phillisa does?" Mo replied.

"Fuck what she believes!" I yelled.

Ashlee moved to sit beside me, and then she put her arms around me. I wanted to shake her off, but I knew her touch was the only thing keeping me from hopping out of my skin.

"You can't lose it with that kid around, Snow," Ashlee whispered in my ear.

Aryanna

I nodded my understanding and took a few moments to pull my shit together.

"So, what's the plan now that we have him? I know you, so I know you can't kill him," Mo stated confidently.

"Don't be so sure," I replied with a sad smile.

"I'm sure enough, now tell me what secrets you have locked away in that beautiful mind of yours," Mo said.

"It's simple, I'm gonna get word to Phillisa that I have her son, and if she wants him back, she's gonna help mount her dad's head on my wall."

"And if she refuses to help?" Ashlee asked.

"Then I'll mount her son's head om my wall," I replied.

My statement left both women silent, but I saw the look they exchanged and it was one of concern.

"Snow?"

I looked to where Chyna was sitting towards the front of the plane, giving her my attention.

"Yeah, what's up, Chyna?"

"Don't kill him. If she doesn't do what you want, just keep him. That'll hurt her more than anything," she replied.

"Chyna's right. Knowing my kids were growing up without me 'bout killed me when I was in prison," Ashlee said.

I didn't respond, because Asad and Lexx picked that moment to reappear from the back of the plane, and I was struck by his infectious smile again.

"Whatchu eating?" I asked.

"I got fruit snacks, and chocolate chip cookies."

"And you didn't bring me any?" I asked, acting as though my feelings were hurt.

He stopped right in his tracks and looked down at the food in his hands. The decision only took a split second because he suddenly thrust both hands at me.

"You can have some of mine," he said.

Despite the ache rolling through my body, I managed to smile genuinely at him, before pushing the food back at him.

"I was just kidding, sweetie. Why don't you take your snacks, and go watch a movie with Chyna?"

"Who's Chyna?" he asked, looking around.

"That would be me, cutie," Chyna replied, raising her hand.

Asad made a beeline for the seat Chyna was occupying and sat down beside her. Once she'd pulled a laptop out of the seat's storage compartment and got settled in with something kid friendly on Netflix, I motioned for Mo, Ashlee, and Lexx to follow me. I led the way to the back of the plane where the bedroom was located, and once we were behind closed doors, I began the planning.

"Alright, now that this phase of things is done, we'll go back home and load up and head to Cuba," I said.

"How are we travelling?" Ashlee asked.

"Boat is the smartest option, since we're only ninety miles away," I replied.

"What about the Coast Guard, don't they patrol international waters heavy for drug runners?" Lexx asked.

"We've got people everywhere, so we'll get a window to slide through," Mo said confidently.

"What type of protection do you think Campa had in Cuba?" Ashlee asked.

"It's best to assume he's heavily guarded, and paying off the government in some way," I replied.

"I'm waiting on an update now from the sources we've tapped to do surveillance," Mo said.

"Call and see if Meatrock has escaped Nicki's clutches yet," I said, looking at Mo.

"So, what's your plan for getting to Campa, if his daughter doesn't agree to betray him for the sake of her son?" Lexx asked.

"I know how Campa works, and he's always looking for new soldiers. It's a habit we both have, so I'm gonna have some people infiltrate his organization the old-fashioned way. Everyone knows it's hard for any drug dealer to make money when bodies are dropping, so I'm gonna drop a few dozen bodies at his feet and see if he pays attention. He'll have the option of either getting rid of the hittas or putting them on his team, and he's never wasted the talents of a good killer," I replied.

"Who are you sending in?" Ashlee asked.

"I'll let you decide that, Ash, since someone in your family makes tactical sense."

She nodded her head in agreement, but she didn't say who she thought was suitable.

"Nicki ain't answering," Mo said.

"Well, call Meatrock then," I suggested.

I waited patiently for her to dial the number and for him to pick up, but when she pulled the phone away from her ear again, I pulled my own phone out. I called Nicki first and when she didn't answer, I called Meatrock. Neither of them answering frustrated the fuck out of me, because I knew they were putting their need to get a nut above business.

"This is why mixing business with pleasure is never a good idea," I said, shaking my head.

I dialed Ashlei's number, hoping that maybe Meatrock was back at her house, but her phone went straight to voicemail.

"Mo, try to call Ashlei and see if she answers for you," I said.

"If she's at work, then she can't answer. You know that," Mo replied.

I felt slightly foolish because this was something that I did know, but I hid my embarrassment and moved on.

"Do you have Fatz's number?" I asked.

"No, there was never a need to have it before now. Don't worry though, we'll be home soon, and in the meantime we should probably all rest, because who knows when we'll get to again," Mo replied.

"You ain't gotta tell me twice," Lexx said, yawning loudly.

"Who's sleeping in the bed?" Ashlee asked, nodding towards the king size mattress that took up most of the space in the room.

"Stop acting like that bed ain't big enough for all of us," Lexx said, wasting no time climbing up on it. Her sister quickly followed her lead, and Mo joined them.

A Dope Boy's Queen 2

They were all looking at me expectantly, but I knew where this shit could go if I got into that bed. Before I knew it, there would be different flavors of pussy on my tongue and fingers, and now wasn't the time for that shit.

"I'm gonna check on Chyna," I said, reaching for the door and disappearing through it before anyone could object.

When I got to the front of the plane, I found Asad watching TV, and the TV watching Chyna, because her ass was knocked out. I moved in silence, but Asad must've felt my presence because his eyes turned on me before I did anything to announce myself. I put a finger to my lips so he wouldn't say or do anything to wake Chyna up. He nodded his head in understanding, which allowed me to take my seat and continue to go over things in my mind.

Knowing what I knew now, I really wanted Phillisa's head more than I did her father's, but I knew I'd have to be patient. Taking her son ensured she would cooperate, and when she proved to be no longer useful, she'd get a closed casket funeral. The thought of that excited me so much, I could feel my pussy getting wet. The feeling of moisture soaking my panties had me looking at the door to the plane's bedroom longingly.

"Do you wanna watch?"

When I turned my head back around, I was surprised to find Asad standing right in front of me, with the laptop balanced in his little hands. I opened my mouth to respond and discovered that I didn't have a voice all of a sudden. I cleared my throat, preparing to try again.

"Uh, okay sure," I mumbled, moving over to make room for him in the loveseat.

He passed me the laptop and climbed up next to me. When he was settled, he held his hands back out for the computer, and I gave it back to him without objection. I watched in awe and fascination as his little fingers navigated the keyboard and brought up an animated movie, I'd seen a million times before.

"You like *Happy Feet*?" I asked.

"Yeah, it's my favorite movie."

"It used to be my son's favorite too," I said smiling.

"You have a son?" he asked, looking up from the screen and into my eyes.

"Yeah, I've got a son."

"Will I get to meet him?"

I gave his question a lot more thought than I thought I would, considering what I was intending to do to him if this shit went sideways. The more I thought about it though, the more another idea formed in my head.

"Maybe one day," I replied smiling.

He smiled back at me, and then went back to watching the best dancing penguin to ever grace the silver screen. Before I knew it, I was quoting the movie right along with him, and laughing too. We watched the entire movie and when it went off, we started it over and watched it again. Sometime during round two, I fell asleep and I stayed knocked out until the pilot announced our approach to the airport.

When I opened my eyes and realized the weight, I was feeling on my stomach was Asad fast asleep, I felt something I'd never expected to. I felt calm. I could feel the smile tugging at my lips, but when I looked up to find Mo sitting across from me, staring at me curiously, I swallowed it.

"Long night?" she asked, smirking.

"Did you get ahold of Nicki or Meatrock?" I asked, changing the topic to business.

"No, not yet, but I sent a message to Red Gunz and told him to contact Fatz. That was about an hour ago."

"Okay. Is everybody else still sleeping?" I asked.

"Yeah…and before you ask, no, I didn't fuck any of them."

"I wasn't gonna ask you no shit like that, Anastasia."

"Good, because I'd hate to fuck you up, bitch," she said smiling.

I chuckled softly, while maneuvering around to put a seatbelt on both me and Asad. Surprisingly, he didn't stir or wake up when I moved him, not even when we touched down a few minutes later and taxied into the private hanger. While Mo went to wake everybody up, I went to have a word with the pilot. We got a quick understanding, and I returned to where Asad lay sleeping.

"You want me to carry him?" Ashlee asked.

"Nah, let him sleep. Listen, I want you all to go back to Ashlei's house, and I'll meet you there when I get back," I said.

"Get back? Uh, bitch, where do you think you're going?" Mo asked, clearly confused and not liking it.

"I'm gonna take him somewhere safe," I replied cryptically.

"We'll go with you," Lexx said.

"No, it's best I do this alone. I trust you all with my life, but this is something I need to do alone. Trust me, I won't be in any danger, and I promise I'm not trying to sneak off so I can hurt him." I said.

The quick look Ashlee and Alexas exchanged told me the thought that I was plotting to kill Asad had crossed their minds almost immediately, but I didn't take offense to it. I could also tell everyone standing here wanted to argue, but they knew me well enough to know how useless that would be. So, without any more fanfare, Ashlee and Alexas went and woke Chyna up, and then they got off the plane. Mo, on the other hand, was still standing in front of me, staring me down like I owed her money.

"What are you doing, Claudette?"

"The right thing."

"And what do you think that is?" she asked slowly.

"I'm taking him to Junior and Alexia."

Hearing those words put an instant smile on her face, and that made me smile too. We hugged each other and exchanged a quick kiss before she got off the plane. I wasted no time going back up front to the pilot and telling him to head back out. Within ten minutes, we'd refueled and were ready to taxi. The roar and whining of the jet's engines was music to my ears, but they suddenly died in mid-crescendo. Before I could go find out what the problem was the door opened, and Mo was running up the stairs.

"Mo, what the fuck—"

"Get off the plane, Claudette."

"Anastasia, I told you I—"

"I know what you said, but we've got a shit show on our hands. Ashlei and Nicki are dead."

Aryanna

Chapter 9

The entire ride from the airport to Ashlei's was a tense one, because we couldn't talk freely with Asad there. I had a million questions, but I hadn't had the opportunity to question anybody yet, and I was growing more pissed by the second. How the hell could Ashlei and Nicki be gone? There had to be some mistake, there just had to be. It took us twenty minutes to get to Ashlei's house, but I still couldn't get the answers I sought right away, because I had to make sure Asad was comfortable in bed. Once that was done, I went to the living room. where I found everybody waiting for me.

"Somebody tell me what the fuck is going on," I said impatiently.

"I don't know what happened to Ashlei, but I was with Nicki last night. I went out to get us something to eat and when I came back, I found Nicki dead, along her three kids. Their skin was peeled off down to their ankles," Meatrock said.

"How fucking long did it take you to go get food, Antonio? I mean, goddamn, you can't skin four fucking people in ten minutes!" I raged.

"I wasn't gone that long, Snow. I went to BeBe's house first and—"

"Just shut the fuck up because if you went to BeBe's house, then there's no telling how long your horny ass was gone," I said, shaking my head in disgust.

BeBe was the only woman Meatrock loved in the world. She was a beautiful young Latina, who just happened to be the mother of his child, and the one that got away. I didn't have a problem with her, but I always knew she'd be his biggest distraction.

"Ashlei got killed at work," Mo said softly.

I turned my attention to her and waited on an explanation.

"There was a riot, and she was one of the hostages that got taken. They-they gang raped her, and slit her throat," Mo said.

Hearing this gave me a moment's pause, because I had real love for Ashlei. I knew death was a very real part of the game we played, but I never wanted any of mine to suffer on their way out. For her to be degraded like that had the rage coursing faster through my veins.

"How did this happen, Mo, when you've both got niggas in there who would die and kill for you?" I asked.

"I don't know, Snow. I—"

"If someone got to Ashlei like that and was able to do what they did, then she was set up," Red Gunz said with certainty.

Vontell and J5 nodded their head in agreement. I knew I had no choice except to take their word, because prison was a world that they were very familiar with. I had no doubt that Nicki could've made a dozen or more enemies in her line of work, but I didn't believe in coincidence. All of this shit was Campa's doing. He wasn't giving up on his mission to kill me and my team, but I damn sure didn't have to wait on him to get here. Without a word, I pulled my phone from my pocket and dialed a number. It took three rings for it to be answered.

"I didn't expect to hear from you, Claudette."

"And you're about to wish you never did. Tell me something, Phillisa, when was the last time you saw your son?" I asked.

"My-my son?"

"Yeah, your son. You know, the one you had by my husband," I said.

"So, you finally figured it out, huh? It doesn't matter though. You can't get to him."

"Are you sure about that? You know I never saw him, and if you believe that's still the case, then how would I know he looks almost identical to my son?" I asked sweetly.

I heard the breath rush from her lungs, and it made me smile. Before she could say anything, I hung the phone up.

"Do you think that was smart?" Ashlee asked.

"Yeah, because I'm tired of this cat and mouse shit. So, now she knows I've got her son and if she's smart, then she'll know what I want," I replied.

"So, what's our next move?" Aubrey asked.

"We still prepare to go to Cuba, because it's the last move Campa might expect me to make," I replied.

"Aubrey, why don't you and Aaron go to the warehouse and pick up the weapons we'll need? From there, you can go straight to the airport, and those of us who are going will meet you there," Mo said.

"Vontrell, I want you and your people to go with them," I said.

"I got you," Vontrell said without hesitation, pulling out his phone.

Aubrey led the way out of the room with the two other men in tow.

"So, are we still gonna try to infiltrate Campa's organization like we talked about?" Ashlee asked me.

"I'm done with subtlety. I want these motherfuckers dead!" I replied, working hard to control my emotions.

"I'm going with you," Meatrock said.

"No, you're not. Somebody had to be here to hold shit down, plus I know you wanna protect BeBe and the kids. I need you here to hold shit down, because God forbid anything happens…you would be destroyed if something happens to BeBe, little Antonio and Yasmin, and I don't want that on my conscience."

I could see on his face that he wanted to argue, but I knew he had to protect the family he and Beatriz had created. After a few moments, he nodded his head in agreement reluctantly.

"Red Gunz, I need you and your people back at the mansion. The cops should be done, but just in case they're not, I'm gonna call and get them out of the way. When you feel like it's safe, I want you to get shipments together for all of our suppliers in Florida. I want you to give them double of whatever their orders usually are," I said.

"Double?" he asked, making sure he heard me correctly.

"Buying loyalty ain't cheap. I need to make sure nobody wants to jump ship right now because of Campa. The threat of violence can be overridden by the power of greed," I replied.

"Facts," he agreed, pulling his phone out and leaving the room.

"Mo, I—"

"I'm on top of it," she said, pulling out her own phone.

Aryanna

I smiled because this was one of the things that I loved about Morano. She knew I needed her to oversee all of these moving parts to make sure they moved together properly. There would never be a substitute for Tony, but Mo was definitely filling his void in a way that I'd be lost without.

"Is my mom here?"

The sound of Asad's voice froze everyone in the kitchen, and had all eyes locked on him, standing in the kitchen doorway.

"Not yet little man, but I just talked to her and she wanted you to know she loves you," I replied.

He came across the room towards me, rubbing the sleep from his eyes. I thought he intended to stand in front of me, but instead he climbed up into my lap and laid against me. I could feel my limbs tighten as sheer panic threatened to override all of my senses, but I fought it. It wasn't like I hadn't been in this position with my own son, it was just…I didn't know how to feel about Zion's illegitimate son. In the end, my motherly instincts won out, and I wrapped my arms around him.

When I did this, he took a deep breath and settled in against me. I looked up to find everyone staring at me, and when I locked eyes with Mo, I could see the tears she was blinking back. I knew the lump I felt in my throat had everything to do with Zion and the love I still felt for him, even as I held the evidence of his betrayal. I now understood why gangsters insisted that they'd never love anything besides the game. Love was beyond any human's control. And it was a weakness to be exploited. So, as much as I loved Zion, I knew I would now exploit that, and his child, for me and my family's survival.

Without a word, I stood up with him still in my arms, preparing to take him back into Ashlei's room. But, before I took a step, the front door to Ashlei's house exploded into tiny wood pieces.

"Move!" I yelled, running from the room.

I quickly stashed a now crying Asad in the hallway bathroom, told him not to move, and pulled my gun out as I stepped back into the hallway. I could already hear the sounds of gunfire coming from the kitchen, so I circled around and came through the living room to join the fun. The lack of a front door made the man dressed in black on the front porch an easy target, and my first two shots separated his head from his shoulders.

"Fatz, hit the lights!" I yelled.

A few seconds later, the house went dark, which made the glowing barrels from the guns barking outside stand out like a fat bitch in the daytime. I took a diving roll out through the front door, coming to a stop right next to some bushes. I wasted no time popping up like a life-size jack-in-the-box and letting my Glock 9mm scream angrily. I dropped two niggas like bad dates, but as soon as I did, it seemed like four more popped up. There were shadowy figures moving all over Ashlei's lawn and in the driveway, but I wasn't scared to be outnumbered. I squeezed off shot after shot until my clip was empty, and then I turned to dive back into the house. What I saw when I turned around froze my blood and breath. In the moonlight, I could make out the tears sliding down Asad's face as he held out his arms to me. Before I could grab him or yell at him to get back inside, his little body was violently thrown back into the darkness.

"No!" I screamed, bolting back inside.

"Snow, are you hit?" Mo called out from my left.

I couldn't find the words to answer because I was scrambling to pull Asad into my arms.

"Hold on, baby boy, I got you," I said, fighting the terror I was feeling.

"Snow!" Mo yelled.

I could hear the panic rising in her voice, but I could also feel blood leaking onto me from the unconscious boy in my arms.

"Asad is hit, we gotta go now!" I yelled.

Moments later, Ashlee and Chyna were beside me, while Fatz, Mo, and Alexas stepped out of the front door with their guns out in front of them.

"They're gonna cover us. You and Chyna go to one of the Lambos, and I'll go to another one. Mo and Fatz will follow us, and Lexx will come with me," Ashlee said.

I didn't answer, I simply waited on them to lay down cover fire so we could move. When I heard the familiar singing of automatic weapons, I followed Ashlee out the door, and made my way to the closest Lamborghini. It wasn't easy to balance Asad in my arms while opening the passenger side door, but I managed to do it.

"Chyna, you drive," I said, sitting down with Asad in my lap.

Bullets were already raining down on the car, making me glad that Mo had had the sense to order them bulletproof. Chyna was behind the wheel within seconds, pushing the button to bring the V-12 engine to life. The other two Lambos were parked behind us, but Chyna didn't wait on them to start their engines.

"Hold on," she said, mashing her foot down hard on the gas pedal.

We lurched forward, and suddenly we were doing a donut in Ashlei's front yard. The sounds of bullets bouncing off the car were quickly drowned out by the loud roar of the engine. I was fighting the G-force that had me thrown deep into the leather seat, but my concern was the fact that Asad still hadn't moved voluntarily.

"Asad, can you hear me?" I asked, pressing my lips to his ear.

He didn't respond, but the warmth of his body kept me hopeful.

"Chyna, I need you to get us to the nearest hospital as fast as you can."

"But what about the questions that will be asked?"

"I don't give a fuck about none of that, all that matters is saving his life," I replied passionately.

I knew how crazy I must've sounded, considering that I'd just been plotting to kill him hours ago, but I didn't care. I was thankful Chyna didn't make me repeat myself either and she was driving the shit out of this car, while managing to use GPS to locate the hospital. When I looked in the side mirror, I saw bright lights following us, but I didn't know if they belonged to friends or enemies. Not having any bullets meant the only thing we had on our side was speed.

"Drive faster, Chyna."

"I'm driving as fast as I can without getting us killed, Snow."

I knew she was telling the truth, so I turned my attention back on Asad.

"Come on, little man, you're gonna be okay," I whispered in his ear.

He still didn't move or give any indication he could hear me, and I could definitely smell the blood oozing from him at this point. If he died now, I knew I'd forever have mixed feelings. Somehow, this little boy had opened me up, and made me feel things that went against my plans. My plans hadn't changed about him being a pawn in life's chess game, but that didn't necessarily mean his life had to be sacrificed. From the moment I felt myself becoming attached, I'd been chewing on a plan in my mind, but if he died in my arms then things would never come together the way I needed.

Thankfully, the hospital was only seven minutes away and before I knew it, we were sliding to a stop in front of the ER. Once the door on my side was up, I quickly wiggled my way out of the car, and hit the ground at a dead run.

"Help! Help me!" I screamed, finally giving in to the panic and terror I felt.

Nurses appeared like magic, talking rapidly and saying things I couldn't understand. It was hard not to resist when Asad was taken out of my arms, but I knew I had to let go so they could help him. I was in hot pursuit of the stretcher they'd put him on, but when they cut his shirt off to check him out, and I saw the huge hole in his chest, I stopped dead in my tracks.

His chest was still rising and falling barely, but I knew grown ass men that couldn't withstand a .44 slug to the chest. I wanted to follow him behind the swinging doors of the operation room, but I couldn't make my feet move. I don't know how long I was standing in that one spot, but the feeling of arms wrapping themselves around me snapped me back to reality.

"He's gonna be okay," Chyna said, laying her head on my shoulder.

"I-I know. He's strong like his father. I need you to do something for me real quick, Chyna."

"Anything, Snow, what is it?"

Aryanna

I pulled my phone out and passed it to her.

"Go take a picture of him," I said.

"Now?"

"Right now," I replied seriously.

She hesitated, but eventually she took the phone I was offering her and disappeared through the double doors in front of me.

"Where is he?" Mo asked, as her and Ashlee came up beside me.

"In the back. He-he got hit in the chest, and it was…"

I couldn't even finish my thought because I was trying to block the visual imagery from my mind.

"Where is Fatz?" I asked, changing the subject.

"He's posted up outside, making sure no one runs up on us. He already sent word we were here, and we needed niggas down here ASAP," Mo replied.

"Where is Meatrock?" I asked.

"He went out of Ashlei's house the back way so he could go get BeBe and the kids. He didn't want them to be sitting ducks in case Campa knows about them," Mo said.

"Make sure he meets us at the airport when he has them, because that's where we're going as soon as Asad comes out of surgery," I said, looking at her.

She nodded her head and pulled out her phone.

"What do you need me to do, Snow?" Ashlee asked.

I looked at her and tried to think of something important for her to handle, but my mind was back with Asad, and the fight for his life. Before I said anything though, Chyna came back through the doors and made her way over to me.

"Where were you?" Ashlee asked.

Chyna didn't respond, she just handed me my phone. I didn't look at the picture she'd taken, but instead selected a recipient for it to be texted to, and I fired it off without a second thought. After that, I started a slow thirty-count that was interrupted by the sound of my phone ringing just eight seconds in.

"Do you understand now?" I asked, answering immediately.

"My-my son! Y-you killed him?"

"No, I didn't. Your father did when he sent his hittas after me and my team. He killed Zion and your son…their blood is on your hands now."

Aryanna

Chapter 10

The sound of the phone disconnecting in my ear was loud, but I'd expected it.

"He's dead?" Mo asked, looking back and forth between me and Chyna.

"No, he's still hanging on and they're operating on him as we speak," Chyna replied.

"But Snow, you just said—"

"I know what I said, and I know why I said it. Either you trust that, or you don't."

"Okay," Mo replied, contritely.

I knew I'd snapped at her, but I didn't have the time nor the inclination to explain myself. Everyone on my team had one job, and that was to remain loyal above all else.

"I thought Fatz was waiting outside," Ashlee said.

I turned around to find Fatz headed in our direction, and he wasn't moving at a leisurely pace.

"What's wrong?" I asked as soon as he got to where we were standing.

"They're here," he replied.

"How the fuck did they follow us?" Chyna asked.

"It doesn't matter. Where's Lexx?" I asked.

Ashlee pointed to the waiting area just out of my vision. My mind was racing, trying to find a solution to what was about to become more than a big ass problem, but I didn't like the only answer that made sense.

"Ashlee, I want you to take Lexx, and find out who flies the medevac helicopter on the roof. Once you find the pilot, I want you up on the roof, and I want those blades spinning ASAP. I don't give a fuck how you do it, just get it done. Fatz, give me a gun, and then I want you and Chyna to post up outside of the operating room," I said.

"What are you gonna do?" Mo asked.

"I'm gonna do what I gotta do, just follow my lead," I replied.

Aryanna

Fatz handed me a Sig Sauer 9mm discreetly, and I quickly slid it into the waist of my jeans. I looked everyone in the eye before turning around and leading the way through the double doors that led to the operating rooms.

"Which one is he in, Chyna?" I asked.

"Second one on the left."

"Post up, and shoot anybody that's a threat," I said, pulling the pistol out and chambering a round.

I kept the gun concealed behind my right leg as I crept into the room.

"Miss, you can't be in here," a nurse said, approaching me quickly with her hands up.

When she got within striking distance, I swiftly raised the gun and let it rest on the bridge of her nose.

"I want all of you to listen to me carefully, so I don't have to repeat myself. That little boy's life is worth more than all of yours, and the family members that you have at home, as far as I'm concerned. So, if you love your life and those on your family tree, you'll do everything you can to save him."

"We-we're doing all that we can, Miss, but you're not helping right now," a tall white man in surgical scrubs replied.

"I'm here because there are people in this hospital right now who want to kill me, that little boy, and everyone else I care about. I've got people guarding the door, but I need you all to stabilize him so we can get him moved before all hell breaks loose," I said.

"You-you can't move him, because—"

"I don't have a choice because if I don't then he dies, and that's unacceptable. So, I advise all of you to work whatever miracles necessary, because you've got minutes to stabilize him, and get him to the helicopter on the roof," I said.

For a second, no one spoke or moved, but then they got back to the hustle and bustle I'd observed when I came in. I lowered the gun away from the nurse's face, but I didn't put it away. She took a step back slowly before turning and going back to doing her job. I wanted to step out into the hall and check on Fatz and Chyna, but I didn't want anyone to get any ideas about alerting the authorities.

A Dope Boy's Queen 2

The sounds and smells of the operating room were testing the sturdiness of my stomach, but I was too much of a gangsta to blow chunks in front of these people.

Thankfully, the team surrounding Asad was blocking his view because there was no way I could watch him fight for his life. Suddenly, the lights flickered as an alarm sounded off somewhere, and then the loudspeaker came on to announce that there was an active shooter inside the hospital.

"Where the fuck do you think you're going?" I asked, levelling my gun at a female nurse who had taken a step away from Asad. "Did you think I was joking when I told you that there were people here to kill us? Well, I wasn't, nor was I bullshitting when I said I'd kill all of you and your families. Now help him!" I said through clenched teeth.

Everyone got back to work with more urgency. I pulled my phone out and called Mo.

"Did you secure the helicopter?" I asked.

"We're waiting on you," she replied.

I hung up, and quickly stuck my head outside the door so that I could see Fatz.

"Get ready to move," I said.

He nodded at me, and Chyna did the same thing. I stuck my head back inside the room and tried to be patient with this process. It wasn't easy though. The sound of gunshots made everyone in the room jump, but I just tightened the grip on my gun.

"Keep working!" I yelled.

The shots were far enough away for me not to be nervous, but close enough that I knew time wasn't on my side. I was not now, nor would I ever be a shaky bitch when it came to getting with the shit, but I could feel the sweat trickling down my back right now. I wasn't afraid for me. I was worried about Asad because he was unable to fight for himself. The only fighting he could do was for his life, and that was where our goals aligned.

"He's stable," the doctor called over his shoulder.

"What's the quickest way to the helipad?" I asked.

"Uh, through the door and to the right," the nurse replied.

Aryanna

"Okay, let's move. I want you and you to come with us," I said, pointing at the doctor and nurse I'd been addressing the whole time.

I could see the fear in their eyes, but they each grabbed one end of the bed and started pushing him towards the door. In total, there were two doctors and the nurse, escorting us to the roof, but my eyes were watching our backs. The sounds of gunshots were getting closer, but we made it to the helicopter without having to shoot anyone.

"Load up!" I yelled over the sound of the rapidly spinning helicopter blades.

Within a matter of moments everyone was inside, and we were taking to the air. In the close quarters of the helicopter, I could no longer avoid seeing Asad, and my heart dropped at what I saw. There was still blood covering his tiny chest, but the hole was covered by a bandage. The thing that really turned my stomach were the tubes running out of him. He looked like a tiny alien from the movie *Independence Day*.

I'd done some things in my life that most people would consider horrible by any stretch of the imagination, and I'd never felt any type of way about it. This situation was causing me to feel things I never had before, and I didn't understand why. I also didn't have the time to psychoanalyze myself to figure shit out either. All I knew was to keep Asad alive, and move on to plan B.

"The pilot wants to know where we're going!" Mo yelled from her seat in the front.

I leaned over and whispered to the doctor to find out if Asad would make it on an out of town flight at this point. He gave a quick shake of his head to say no, which only left me one option.

"Tell him to get us to the closest hospital!" I yelled back.

I saw her relay my message, and the pilot nod his head in compliance. There was a serious risk to what I was doing, which meant I had to minimize it somehow. I pulled my phone out and googled the nearest hospital, and then I sent a group text to have all my soldiers meet us there. I needed the hospital locked down to avoid a repeat of what had just happened. I had to get Asad healthy enough to fly.

It took us twenty minutes to arrive at the hospital, and they rushed Asad straight back into surgery. I didn't have to pull my gun back out because the fear and understanding was still in the eyes of the doctors' and the nurse that had come with me, and that allowed me to step back while they worked. I didn't wait in the waiting room with Ashlee, Mo, Chyna, and Lexx, nor did I wait in the hallway with Fatz. I was posted up in the ER like a necessary piece of equipment. It was a full three hours later before the doctor removed his gloves and mask and turned towards me.

"He's an incredibly strong little boy, and he's managed to fight this far, but there are no guarantees. Even though I know what we just left at the hospital, I still have to ask you if it's absolutely necessary for you to travel with him?"

"Trust me, Doc. If it weren't, then I wouldn't do it," I replied.

I could see he was wrestling with something internally, but I had no idea what it could be.

"Can I speak with you in private for a moment?" he asked me.

I nodded my head and led the way out into the hallway. When we got there, I led him far enough away from Fatz that he couldn't overhear, and then I turned to the doctor expectantly.

"I don't know why you've got people gunning for you and an innocent little boy, and to be honest, it's not my business or concern. What is my concern is that he survives through the night, so I have a proposition for you."

"Which is?" I asked.

"Wherever you're going, I'd like to go with you."

"That's a noble gesture, Doc, but I don't think that's a good idea for your life's expectancy," I replied honestly.

"Be that as it may, I took an oath as a doctor and I'm bound by it."

I stared at him for a moment to gauge just how serious he was, and the determination I saw in his blue eyes actually surprised me. This wasn't at all a part of my plans, so I had no idea why I was considering it, but I was.

"Doc, it could take him a while to recover from this, if he recovers at all. You can't just go missing without people noticing."

"Actually, I can. I live alone, and I have no family on this side of the country. I can and will take a vacation from work, so that won't be a problem either," he replied.

Despite him having an answer to all the problems I'd laid out I was still hesitant to agree to what he was suggesting. The real issue was the amount of time I was wasting at this very moment, because I definitely had a war to get back to.

"Tell you what, Doc. I'll agree to what you're suggesting, but only if you allow me to pay you. I know you're not doing it for the money, but I'll feel better if it's business instead of a favor."

"Fair enough, but I do have one request."

"And what's that?" I asked.

"My name is Kevin."

"Okay, Kevin. Are you ready to go?" I asked.

"Whenever you are."

He led me back into the operating room, where he gave directions for Asad to be transported back to the roof where the chopper was waiting. I rounded up the troops and within ten minutes, we were airborne once again. I made sure my ground troops repositioned themselves at the mansion, because we were definitely coming in hot. Meatrock, BeBe, and their kids were already there waiting on us, which meant we could get going as soon as the helicopter touched down.

The flight took an uneventful thirty minutes, but I knew once we landed, there would be some type of fireworks. The first priority once we touched down was getting Asad settled in. While Kevin checked and double-checked everything, I had my team wait for me on the tarmac so we could talk.

"Listen, it goes without saying that I love you all, but I need to do this by myself," I said.

"What the fuck are you talking about, Snow?" Mo asked, with obvious irritation.

"I'm talking about you all staying here. I can handle the next move alone."

"I know damn well you didn't go through all that shit to save that boy's life just so you could have the pleasure of killing him," Ashlee said.

"Nah, it's not like that," I replied, shaking my head.

"Then what's it like, bitch, because this cryptic bullshit is getting old real quick," Mo said, putting her hands on her hips.

"It's simple. Phillisa thinks her son is dead, and her father is the one responsible. That just made her an ally. So, we're gonna work with her to cut the head off of the more deadly snake. That plan doesn't exactly work if her son is somewhere where she can get to him, so I'm gonna hide him. It's best if no one knows where."

I could tell by the looks I was receiving that everyone felt some type of way, but I didn't act like I didn't know why. To them I'd basically said I didn't trust them, but that wasn't the case. I just wanted to do this alone, to minimize the amount of mistakes that could lead to a death I couldn't live with.

"I'll be back by tomorrow morning, I promise," I said.

"Whatever, bitch," Mo said, shaking her head in disgust.

"I will be, that's my word. Take Meatrock's car and go to the mansion. Mo, I'm counting on you to make sure everything is in order because when I come back, I'm sure Phillisa won't be too far behind. Get everybody in position and send some people to Cuba so we've got eyes on the ground. I'm leaving you in charge," I said.

She didn't reply, but she nodded her head in understanding. I hated to leave my team behind, but I was in charge because I accepted the responsibility of making the hard decisions. That understanding is what allowed me to turn around and make my way up the stairs onto the plane.

"Let's go," I said, taking my seat.

"Where is everyone else?" Meatrock asked.

They're not coming with us. The only reason you're going is because I need you there to protect everyone," I replied.

"Who exactly is everyone, and where the hell are we going?"

"You'll see," I said, picking up the phone next to the leather seat I was sitting in. I made the call and told the pilot to take off. Once Meatrock heard the destination I gave the pilot, he sat down beside BeBe, and focused on her. I could only assume their kids were in the back bedroom sleeping. As the plane came to life with a roar bigger than any lion's, Kevin finished up securing Asad's bed a few feet away. When that was taken care of, he sat beside me and strapped in. A few minutes later we were actually in the air, and I breathed a sigh of relief.

"Can I ask you a question?" Kevin asked.

"You kinda just did," I replied.

"You know what I mean."

"What is it, Kevin?" I asked, sighing deeply.

"Does this have anything to do with your job?"

"My-job," I replied, genuinely confused for a moment.

"Yes, your job. Or do you think that I didn't recognize you, counselor?"

For a moment he had me at a complete loss of words because in all honestly, I'd somehow lost sight of the legal shit I was into.

"I didn't realize that I was someone to be recognized, but to answer your question, I guess you could say it's a mixture of business and personal."

"I can see that, because whoever that little boy is, he means a great deal to you. You're a well-respected and successful lawyer, and that's what kept my coworkers calm back there. We understood that what you were doing was out of love and fear, and that was something we could relate to on some level. Maybe not to that extreme, but still."

"I appreciate the sympathy," I replied.

"So, do you wanna talk about what got you in this situation?"

"Nope," I replied, laying back in the seat.

"Oh…well okay, I'm here if you ever want to talk though."

I nodded my head before closing my eyes. I concentrated hard on clearing my mind of all the excess noise and drama and focused on what would come next. I locked in on those thoughts until I was unconscious and sleeping deeply. I didn't dream, but I woke up feeling more peaceful than I had a right to feel. I opened my eyes to find everyone else sleeping peacefully as the plane glided down out of the clouds.

A Dope Boy's Queen 2

When we hit the runway, I pulled my phone out and called for my people to come pick us up. The plane taxied into a private hanger where we sat and waited for about fifteen minutes, until three identical black Suburban's pulled into the hanger.

I woke everybody up, and the first order of business was getting Asad into a truck, without disturbing his IV or hurting him. Once that was done, everyone else loaded up and we moved out. The drive took us more than an hour because we had to travel up into the mountains, but the spectacular view was worth it.

"Why here?" Kevin asked.

"Because it's nothing like where I come from," I replied honestly.

We pulled up to the huge house I'd bought, and before the trucks had stopped rolling good, I saw the front door to the house open. I hopped out and braced for impact.

"Mom!"

Aryanna

Chapter 11

"I'm gonna need you to stop growing if you're gonna run up on me like that," I said, trying to catch my breath while squeezing my son tightly.

"I'm sorry, Mom, but I've missed you. Can I come home yet?" he asked, pulling back to look up into my face.

I could see the hope in his eyes, and it hurt my heart to know I had to tell him no.

"Honestly, sweetheart, I need you to stay here a little longer so you can help me out."

The frown that covered his face was instantaneous, but I quickly smoothed the wrinkles out of his little forehead with endless kisses.

"M-Mom, stop it," he said, giggling and squirming in my arms.

I ignored him of course and kept right on kissing him.

"Okay-okay, I give in!" he was yelling, laughing harder.

I pulled him to my chest and just held him for a moment, while inhaling his scent. I couldn't put into words how much I'd missed my baby boy, but the tears I felt sliding down my cheeks said it all.

"So how long are you staying, Mom?"

"I have to be back in Florida for court tomorrow, but I really needed to see you," I replied.

I hated to mix truth with lie, but the real truth would come out soon enough.

"So, only today?"

"The amount of time doesn't matter, Junior, only the memories made in that time. Now where is Alexia and her family?" I asked.

"Inside."

"Okay, well show me around," I said, wiping my face.

He stepped out of my arms and grabbed my hand, before leading the way inside. I looked back at the trucks sitting in the driveway and signaled for everyone to unload, while Junior was distracted. I'd bought the split level, eight-bedroom house once I'd realized I needed somewhere safe and somewhat permanent to hide Junior, but I'd never actually been out here to see it.

Aryanna

From the moment I walked through the door, I had the impression I was at a ski resort for the rich and famous. The open floor plan and glass ceiling gave the feeling that I could touch the clouds, or ski on them if I do desired. The rosewood color scheme gave a warm and inviting feeling, and the sound of the fire crackling nearby only added to it. I could smell hot chocolate in the air, and it took my mind back to when I used to make it for Junior when he was a little kid.

"Hi, Mrs. Snow," Alexia said, smiling as she walked over and gave me a hug.

"Hi, Alexia, it's good to see you."

"You too. My mom is in the kitchen," she said.

"Lead the way," I replied.

She turned back in the direction she'd come from, and both Junior and I followed her.

"Hey, Claudette, I wasn't expecting you," Vivianna said, wiping her hands on her apron.

"Something came up, and I needed to talk with you face-to-face. Plus, I missed my mini-me," I said, pulling Junior close to me.

"Well, I know he's missed you, because I get the question every day about when we're going back to Florida," Vivianna said, smiling and shaking her head.

"Yeah, I know you're all probably home sick. There's only so much skiing you can do."

"I learned how to snowboard too, Mom," he informed me proudly.

"That's good, sweetie, and you get to be my teacher," I replied.

"Okay, let's go," he replied, pulling me by the hand towards the back door.

"Why don't you go get dressed in your snowsuit while I talk with Vivianna real quick. Take Alexia with you."

I could tell he didn't wanna let my hand go even for a second, and that made my heart beat faster. My little man might have been growing up, but he still loved me with everything in him, and I needed that.

"Alexia, look in my closet and find something warmer for Junior's mom to wear," Vivianna said.

"Okay, Mom."

They left the room together, but I still waited until they were out of eavesdropping range before speaking.

"I need your help, Viv."

"Yeah, I figured as much, because you look like shit."

"Thanks. Come with me," I said, turning and going back to the front door.

I opened it in time to prevent Meatrock from knocking and alerting everyone else to what was going on.

"I need a room, Viv," I said, looking over my shoulder at her.

She nodded her head and turned towards the hallway. I motioned for Kevin and the niggas pushing Asad to follow us. Vivianna never turned around until we were in the bedroom she'd chosen, but when she did, her eyes got as big as softballs.

"Who-who is that?" she asked.

"Look at him closely," I said, taking a step back.

She was hesitant to take any steps forward, but she eventually did.

"He looks like—"

"I know, and there's a story to go behind it, but right now ain't the time. I need you to keep him here where it's safe, and the doctor is gonna stay with you," I said.

"My name is Kevin," he said, maneuvering the bed into the room.

He went about setting everything up while we watched in silence.

"Snow what's going on back home," Vivianna asked, looking at me.

"We're at war, and it's ugly," I admitted.

"Is-is Fatz—"

"Nah, he's good. You know the type of nigga he is, so this is his lane," I said smiling.

"I know I'm married and Alexia has a stepfather, but I still care about Fatz a lot. He's one of the good ones, so don't get him killed."

"I got you…just take care of Asad for me," I replied.

"It's what his father would want," Vivianna said, giving me a knowing look.

I gave her a sad smile, which made her step forward and hug me. We embraced until the familiar sound of running footsteps could be heard.

"Kevin, I want you to take care of Asad, and I'll pay you when I bring you home," I said.

"Will do."

"Come on, Viv, I've gotta figure out how to explain this shit to Junior," I said.

I led the way out of the room, and back to the kitchen. I found the kids sneaking cookies to go along with their hot chocolate.

"Look at you, caught red-handed," I said, laughing.

The look on their faces was priceless, and it made me laugh harder.

"Before we go snowboarding, Junior, I need to have a conversation with you. Come with me," I said, holding my hand out.

He came to me without hesitation, and I took his hand in mine. I led him down the hallway to the bedroom I'd put Asad in, and I stopped right outside the door.

"Junior, I need to tell you something, and I need you to be a big boy about it."

"Mom I am a big boy, so we really don't have to have the talk. Besides, I've seen everything on YouTube anyway."

"Wait, what? What the hell are you talking about, boy?" I asked, looking at him like he was crazy.

He gave me a sheepish smile as the skin on his cheeks heated up and changed colors.

"I, uh… I thought you were t-talking about—"

"Hell no, I wasn't talking about no damn sex, and you better keep that little dick in your pants, or I'll snatch it straight off your body! Understand?"

"Yes, ma'am," he replied softly.

I spent another few seconds staring at him to drive my point home. I hadn't been wondering what he'd been out here doing with

Alexia, but now my mind was spinning. I had to push it to the side though and focus on what I came to do.

"Junior, you know I love you, right?"

"I know, Mom."

"And I've always told you how much your dad loves you too. None of that will ever change."

"Mom, what's wrong?" he asked, looking me up and down curiously.

"I'm fine, I'm fine. It's just that I recently found something out that is gonna change our lives forever," I said.

"What is it?"

I opened my mouth to say Asad's name, but only air came out. I had no idea how to say what needed to be said, so I did the only thing I could think to do. I opened the bedroom door and stepped aside. Junior looked at me with eyes full of questions, but he didn't move from the spot he was standing in.

"It's okay, baby, go ahead," I urged.

He glanced in the room, and then looked at me again. I nodded my head, and that got his feet moving. I locked eyes with Kevin, and I could see the worry written all over his face. There was really no other way to handle this though. When Junior saw the hospital bed, he turned around and looked at me, but I motioned for him to keep going. His feet slid soundlessly across the wooden floor, but that only made the gasp that escaped his lips louder.

"M-M-Mom," he whispered.

I was by his side in an instant, putting my hands on his shoulders.

"Who is-is he, Mom?"

"He's your brother."

"How?" he asked.

His question was so innocent, but the complications that came with the answer were staggering.

"If you've been watching YouTube, then I don't really need to explain how this is possible," I replied.

"I mean no, but...he's younger than me."

"I know, sweetie," I said.

Aryanna

When he turned around to face me, I knew he could see the pain I was desperate to hide.

"He still loved us, Junior," I said, pulling him towards me. He held onto me tightly, and I could feel his little body shaking against mine. I didn't know if he was crying or if he was just that mad, but it didn't matter because I was here. I held him until I felt him stop trembling, and then I pulled back so I could look down at him.

"I promise you that your dad loved us, Junior, but sometimes things happen. I don't want you ever questioning your dad's love."

"I won't, Mom, but...what happened to him, my brother I mean?"

"I don't want you to worry about that, I just want you to do me a favor and help take care of him. Can you do that for me?" I asked.

"Yeah. I know how important family is."

His response made me smile and hug him again.

"I'm gonna push my court date back a day so we can spend some time together."

I kissed the top of his head, and then led him from the room. We met up with Alexia and Vivianna in the kitchen, where I was given a snowsuit.

"I hope you're ready to freeze your ass off," Vivianna said smiling.

I shook my head in resignation while accepting the suit, and the inevitable. I wasn't going through it alone though, so I made everyone in my entourage hit the slopes with us. We spent the entire day doing something carefree and foreign, while trying to put the blood on our hands out of our minds. The sound of my son's laughter was like balm for my soul, and it was more precious than the air filling my lungs.

We had so much fun, I completely forgot to notify Mo that I had changed plans. So, when our dinner was interrupted by the notification that another SUV was pulling up, I already knew who was inside. I excused myself and walked out front to meet her, and hopefully calm her down.

"Mo, I know I said—"

"You promised, bitch, but I'm not here for that. Where's my nephew?"

I didn't say anything, I just led her back inside and made her a plate of food. Of course, Junior was happy to see another familiar face, so there was no awkward tension. I thought that at some point during the evening, I'd have to have a conversation with Mo, but the more time she spent with us, I could tell she understood my moves and motive.

Later that night when Junior was fast asleep in the bed beside me, she came into the room, and laid on the other side of him. We communicated with our eyes only, but I felt the love and comfort she'd come to give. I fell asleep staring at her and was blessed enough to wake up with her still there.

Once everyone was up, we spent our day much like we had the first one. The seconds, minutes and hours slipped by so effortlessly, when Mo informed me that it was time to go back home, I was truly shocked. I could see the heartbreak written all over Junior's face, and I tried not to let him see my own pain. I felt so bad that I took him with me to the airport so he could say goodbye from there. We hugged each other as if we'd never see each other again, and when I let him go, he hurried back to the truck.

"Meatrock, I'm trusting you in a way I've never had to before. Don't let me down, bruh," I said seriously.

"I'll protect them just like they were my own, but what exactly is your plan, Snow?"

"Right now, the plan is to be the last one standing when the smoke clears. As for Phillisa's son...he died. That's Zion's son back there fighting for his life, and I'll treat him accordingly," I replied.

My response brought no more questions, so we hugged quickly and I boarded the plane.

"You okay?" Mo asked.

"Nah, not really," I admitted softly.

I sat down beside her and put my head in her lap. She stroked my hair lovingly as I closed my eyes, and let the tears silently slide. The hurt outweighed the anger for a moment, making me question if I would survive even after the killing was done. I knew I had to mentally fortify myself for what was coming, but it was harder to do that than ever before.

"We're gonna get through this, bitch," Mo said softly.

"How can you be so sure?"

My question caused her to flip me over onto my back, so she could stare down into my face.

"It might seem like this shit is the worst shit we've been through, but it's not. We've been to hell and back, lost a lot of people we love, but we're still standing, and do you know why?"

"Why?" I asked.

"Because real bitches like us can't be broken that easily. That's the truth Campa and his bitch ass daughter chose to overlook, and that'll be their undoing. Mark my words."

"I hope you're right," I said.

"Just in case I'm not, let's put a plan together. Come on," she said, pushing me up and off of her. I thought we were going to the back of the plane, but instead she pulled me into the seat next to her and strapped on my seatbelt. We waited for everyone to load up and strap in, and then the plane taxied for takeoff. Once we were climbing steadily through the clouds, Mo tapped me on the arm, and motioned for me to follow her. I undid my seatbelt and followed her.

When she led me into the office, I thought we were about to discuss strategy, but as soon as the door closed, I found my back pressed against it and her lips were on me. If I'd wanted to breathe anything other than her tongue, it would've been impossible, but the fire in my gut told me I was good with that. I kissed her back with the same unchecked passion, pulling at her clothes the whole time. I needed to feel her skin beneath my fingertips and once I did, the heat I felt only made me hotter.

"Fuck me!" I demanded.

She wasted no time pulling my pants and panties to my ankles and pulling one leg completely free. Before I had time to brace, she had my leg thrown up over her shoulder, and she was giving some great mouth-to-mouth to my pussy lips. I grabbed a handful of her hair and hung on tight, while I let the beat of my orgasm build.

"Mo-Moooooooo!" I cried out as she sucked hard on my clit.

I could feel the vibrations of her laughter rocket through my pussy and tingle all the way up to my eyebrows. Within minutes, I had to clamp my hands over my mouth so everybody on the plane wouldn't hear me cumming. The intensity of my climax was so overwhelming, I literally bit my tongue until I could taste my own blood fill my mouth. I didn't care though. I was too busy smiling like a damn fool. After she had her fill of drinking from me, she stood up and kissed me tenderly.

"Is it my turn now?" I asked, caressing her breasts softly.

"Maybe later. Right now, we really do need to figure out our next ten moves."

I could tell she was serious, and I almost let her off the hook. Almost. Before she could straighten her clothes, I grabbed her, spun her around, and pushed her face down on the wooden desk sitting in the corner.

"Snow, we need to—"

Her words got stuck somewhere behind her tongue when I kneeled behind her and started eating her pussy from the back. My tongue was playing double dutch with her pussy lips, at the same time it was playing tag with her clit. The end result was her holding onto the desk for dear life.

"Oh fuck," she whined, while attempting to run from my assault.

I held onto her hips and forced her to surrender her free will to me. I moved my hand to her ass and pushed my finger inside her asshole, while flickering my tongue back and forth across her clit with the speed of a strobe light. The result of my work came almost instantaneously in the form of her pussy opening like a beautiful underground spring, gushing all of her sweetness into my mouth. I took all that she had to give me, and only then did I back away from her trembling body.

"So, what did you wanna discuss?" I asked, putting my clothes back on.

"F-fuck you, bitch, I need a minute."

I laughed genuinely while shaking my head and buttoning my pants. I waited patiently while she caught her breath and fixed her clothes. When she was done, she turned around to face me, but before she could say anything my phone started ringing. I pulled it out and answered it while still smiling a satisfied grin at her.

"Yeah?"

"Snow, where are you?" Fatz asked.

The panic in his voice erased my smile quickly.

"On the way back, why?"

"The mansion got blown up…and there were cops inside," he said.

"What?"

"You heard me! And they're saying it's your fault."

A Dope Boy's Queen 2

Chapter 12

The glow from my orgasm faded quicker than a dying fire, and my mind was focused on what to do when we hit the ground. It was hard to put a plan together when I couldn't assess the damage for myself. All Fatz had been able to tell me was that for some reason, the feds had shown up at the mansion and sometime after that, the house exploded. All of this had taken place while I'd been on the slopes, and thankfully Fatz had been out taking care of business. Some of the people on my team hadn't been so lucky. The moment we touched down, I demanded to be taken to the mansion so I could see what was left.

"It looks like a bomb went off," I said.

"As best as we can tell, it was at least three RPG's, probably from different angles," Fatz replied.

Looking at the wreckage, I could see how that conclusion was reached. There was barely anything left of the house's structure, which gave it a haunted appearance. In my heart, I felt like the people we'd lost would forever haunt me.

"Where are Aubrey and Aaron?" I asked.

"At one of the new properties with Chyna, trying to console her," he said.

I didn't know how I'd look at any of them the same, now that Ashlee and Alexas were gone. Their deaths were on my hands, and I'd die knowing that. The feeling of Mo's hand on my shoulder brought little comfort, but I didn't shake her off.

"Do we have any idea why the feds were here?" I asked.

"I don't know for sure, but I don't think it was official business. There's not a record of a planned raid, or an undercover mission being sanctioned," he replied.

"Is that nigga really so bold as to send the feds to get his dope?" Mo asked in disbelief.

"I don't put anything past that crazy motherfucker," I said.

"Well, if he did, then he'd be a day late and a dollar short."

"What are you talking about Fatz?" I asked, looking over at him.

111

The smile he gave me told me he was up to no good. He didn't answer my question though, he just put the truck in gear and pulled off. We rode in silence for twenty minutes, until we came to a storage unit in a part of town that I wasn't familiar with.

"Come on," Fatz said, hopping out.

Mo and I followed him out, and inside the building to the last unit. When he unlocked the lock and lifted the door, I stared into the darkness, waiting for an explanation.

"Alexa, lights on," Fatz commanded.

When the room was suddenly lit, I understood the smile on Fatz's face.

"What made you move everything?" I asked, looking at him.

"It just seemed like the smart move, given the police activity at the mansion, especially since business still has to be done. So, when Red Gunz did what you told him, I told him to help me make this move."

I turned my eyes on Mo and smiled slightly.

"Your nigga is smart," I said.

"This is what I know, bitch," she replied.

"I know that this doesn't fix the biggest problem, but it keeps the lights on," Fatz said.

"Nah, but it's time I did my part," I said, pulling out my phone, and leading the way back out to my truck.

I hopped in the passenger seat while dialing a number and waiting on it to be answered.

"Claudette?"

"We need to talk, Phillisa," I said.

"About what?"

"Stop playing, bitch, and tell me where you're at," I said frustrated.

"Why would I do that, so you can kill me like you did my son?"

"I told your ass the last time we talked, I didn't kill your son, your father did. Are you trying to straighten that, or nah?"

My question was met with silence, but I was sure she was just thinking.

"I'm in Cuba," she said.

"Stay by your phone, I'll be there soon," I replied, disconnecting the call.

"Where is she?" Mo asked.

"Cuba," I said.

I could hear Mo dialing a number as she got into the truck, and seconds later she was ordering for the plane to me fueled and ready. I sent a text message to Aubrey and asked him if they were going with us. While waiting on the response to that, I fired off texts to Vontrell and J5 to meet us at the warehouse in one hour. When Fatz got back behind the wheel, I told him what the next destination was, and he got us on the move. While he drove, I reached out to any and everyone I could think of to take with me to war, but I was coming up empty-handed.

"Mo, I can't reach any of our normal people to ride into the unknown with us. Try your hand."

"I got you," she replied.

With her on top of that, I focused on reaching out to the political contacts I'd made over the years. The list of favors that were owed to me was extensive, but I didn't know if they could reach the shores of Cuba. By the time we made it to the warehouse, I had assurances that I could land in Cuba armed with everything short of a nuclear weapon. There was a catch, of course.

"We've only got twenty-four hours on Cuban soil, and then our citizenship will be revoked in a violent way," I said.

"Well then, we gotta move fast, and whatever we do had to be done with the team we have because I got nowhere," Mo said.

"Phillisa will have men with her," I replied.

"Yeah, and they'll be loyal to her, not us, which means we can look forward to some shit shaking after Campa is dead," Fatz said.

"She'll be dead before then," I said, opening my door and getting out.

When I walked into the warehouse, about thirty sets of eyes turned on me, and all conversation stopped. I waited until Mo and Fatz walked in before I addressed the crowd.

"My family is under attack, which means you're under attack. Instead of waiting to die, it's time that we bring some death to their door. Anybody not with that is free to walk away," I said.

No one moved, and the look on Aubrey and Aaron's faces told me this was exactly where they wanted to be.

"Alright then, let's load up all of these weapons and get gone," I said.

Everyone started to move around, and Fatz took the initiative to organize the loading process. We were loading down two panel vans with all types of artillery, but I still wasn't about to underestimate Campa. There was no telling what the fuck he had waiting for us.

"Snow, I need you to do me a favor," Aubrey said, walking over to me.

"Anything, Aubrey."

"I need you to find somewhere safe to keep Chyna. I need you to find somewhere beyond this motherfucker's reach to put my last remaining sister, because I can't lose her too. You owe us that," he said.

I didn't take any offense to his statement, because I blamed myself for what happened just as much as he did.

"I got her, Aubrey, I give you my word. I'll send someone to get her now and move her to the safest place in the world," I replied.

He nodded before turning and walking away.

"Mo."

"I got it, Claudette," she said, pulling her phone back out.

I left that problem in her capable hands while I pulled my own phone out and called for our ride.

"We'll be ready within the hour," I said.

The response was one word, and then I hung up. I walked around the warehouse and watched with hawk eyes while the weapons were loaded up.

"Are you ready for this?" Mo asked, trailing behind me.

"Absolutely. What about you?"

"As ready as one can be for this shit to jump off," she replied honestly.

"I know what you mean. It'll all be over soon."

"Will it though, Claudette?"

The way she asked the question made me stop in my tracks and turn to face her.

"What's that supposed to mean?"

"It means this is the life you chose, so look around because there's no way out when you're in this deep," she replied.

My response was a lie that wasn't worthy of telling, so I kept it to myself and went back to inspecting. A half an hour later, everything was loaded up, and we were on the move.

"Are the plane's ready?" I asked Mo.

"Yeah, and Chyna is already on board. She wanted to know if she could stop and pick up her baby, and her sister's kids?"

"That's not smart. They're not a target, but she could make them one if someone somehow finds them. I can't take the risk that she might lead people to that location."

"Understood," Mo said.

I didn't feel good saying what I did, but it was the harsh truth. I loved Chyna and her family like they were my own, but I couldn't put them ahead of my own. I just couldn't. It took us twenty minutes to get to the marina, and another thirty to load the boat.

"Are we good to go, Captain Medina?" I asked.

"We are."

"Okay. Mo, I want you to tell both planes to take off," I ordered.

I knew Campa was smart enough to be watching the airports and private landing strips for unannounced planes, so I'd sent a jet to Cuba as a diversion. Thanks to my connections, I would arrive on Cuban soil courtesy of the Coast Guard. This would allow me to kill two birds with one stone because now I didn't have to sneak around the law, at least not the law I was familiar with. Once we put boots on the ground, I was more or less on my own, but I wasn't worried. I was determined.

We were travelling on a boat big enough to hold my entire team, but there was still a second boat that followed us across the ocean. Ninety miles of dark blue water was all that separated me from my goal, and we were moving fast towards it.

Aryanna

"Five minutes out!" the captain yelled a couple hours later, over the cutter's engines.

We didn't pull into any port like a legally docking ship when we arrived, we made land fall on a beach not far from Guantanamo Bay Prison. We rendezvoused with some guerrillas that were being paid as tour guides, loaded our weapons into their trucks, and moved to the safehouse right outside the city of Havana.

While everyone else was getting settled and catching a few hours of sleep I was up, pacing and thinking. The restlessness coursing through my veins was irritating me, and it eventually made me sit down so that I could meditate. I focused all my thoughts and energy on Zion and tried to see all of this through his eyes. I felt emotionally disconnected from his memory because of all that had happened, but I still tried channeling the war god in him.

A lot of bad could be said about my late husband, but I knew more of the good than anyone else. In this instance, his ability to kill without remorse was a good thing for me to remember, because at the end of the day, I had to do the same thing. I pulled out my phone and dialed the number that always made me throw up in my mouth a little.

"Do you know what time it is, Claudette?"

"Time to wake up, Phillisa. We've got shit to do."

"You're here already?"

"You sound surprised. Did you think I was bullshitting when it came to killing your father?" I asked.

"No, I know that you're serious as I am."

"Oh, so now you're serious about it, huh?"

My question left her silent, but I could still hear her breathing in my ear. Part of me took extreme pleasure from the pain I was causing her, because I felt like she deserved it for fucking with my family. There was a small part of me though, the mother in me, that felt bad for lying about something so serious.

"I blame you for my son's death, Claudette, because you put him in danger. If you would've left him in Columbia, then he...he'd be safe. I know you didn't pull the trigger though. That doesn't excuse what you did do, but you and I will deal with that later."

"On that we agree, because if you think that any of this excuses the fact that you fucked my husband, then you got me all the way fucked up!" I growled, growing angrier.

"You need to stop acting like Zion was innocent in all of this shit. I didn't rape him bitch, we had sex, and he wanted it as much as I did! So cut the dumb shit out like Zion was a victim."

"No, I'm the victim! My son that has to grow up without his father is the goddamn victim! So, don't come at me like it was just sex because you not keeping your motherfucking legs closed is what has us in this current situation, you trifling bitch!"

I could hear her anger in how hard she was breathing on the other end of the phone, but I gave no fucks. The facts were the facts. I let her stew in her feelings for a few seconds before bringing it back to the topic at hand.

"Are you ready to do this or not?" I asked.

"I'm sending you the location and layout of Campa's compound, which is in the center of the city. Me and my people will attack from the east, and you attack from the west. Simultaneous action is the only way to throw him off balance and give us the advantage. Call me when you're in position," she said, hanging up.

No sooner had I pulled the phone away from my ear it started vibrating with an incoming text message. I looked over the images that she'd sent me, studying the angle that me and my people would strike from. I shot Phillisa a text back, assuring her we would be in position by dawn. After that, I sent Mo a text for her to come to my room. Within seconds, she was walking through the door.

"I've got the layout of Campa's compound."

"How heavily guarded is it?" she asked, sitting beside me on the bed.

I passed her my phone so she could see for herself.

"I'm assuming the red arrows signify where he has people positioned," she said.

"It looks that way."

"Well, I guess if it was easy, then everyone would try to kill El Jefe," she said, shaking her head.

"Phillisa is gonna attack one side at the same time as we're attacking the other."

"Are you sure about that, Snow?"

I could see the concern in her eyes, and it matched some of the fear churning in my stomach.

"There's no doubt in my mind that she still wants to kill me, but her father is her priority for the moment," I replied.

"And when that's taken care of?"

"Then whoever has a clear shot better take it, or we'll be right back at war with a highly motivated opponent," I replied sincerely.

Mo nodded her understanding while continuing to study the pictures on my phone.

"So, when do we hit him?" she asked.

"Right before dawn."

"Because it's darkest before the dawn?" she asked, looking up at me.

"Fitting, isn't it?" Her smile was answer enough.

We spent about an hour talking strategy, and then we called Fatz, Red Gunz, Vontrell, Aubrey, Aaron, and J5 in to join the discussion.

"Going full throttle is the only way to play this," Gunz said.

"All go, and no whoa," Vontrell said, nodding in agreement.

"I think we can all agree on that. Once we get rid of the lookouts and guards, we need to split up so we can cover every inch of his compound as quick as possible," I said.

"Like ants at a picnic," Aubrey said, nodding in agreement.

"Exactly," Mo replied.

"There's no need to wait when it comes to killing Phillisa either, so once we know Campa is dead, we move on her. Here's what she looks like," I said, passing my phone around the room.

Everyone got a look at the picture, hopefully computing it to memory, because missing her wasn't an option. Once I got my phone back, I looked at Mo.

"If any one of you doesn't make it out of this, your family's will be taken care of. You have my word," Mo said.

"Any question?" I asked, searching each and every face for any uncertainty.

I saw none, and that gave me more confidence.

"Alright then, let's get the weapons and go. Today is as good a day as any to kill somebody," I said smiling.

Aryanna

Chapter 13

"On my count, Claudette. Three…two…one."

I hung up the phone and gave Fatz the signal. He wasted no time firing the rocket at the west wall, and by the time the rocket landed, the east wall was exploding. Fatz stepped out of the way, and Aubrey stepped forward with the grenade launcher and let it fly. The ground shook violently again, and the sound of screams rang out louder than any church bells.

"Let's go," I said, stepping out from behind the van with my AR-15 at eye level.

We crept from out of the shadows, making a beeline for what was left of Campa's hideout.

"On the roof," Fatz said.

I raised my gun and squeezed off three shots that made the body fall from the sky. There was no pulse in my steps as I entered through what remained of the kitchen. The sound of rapidly spoken Spanish caught my attention, and I turned in time to fire a shot that lifted a man's thoughts out of his head. I stepped over his body, and around the bodies of two female housekeepers, making my way towards the sounds of gunfire. I waited for Mo to come up next to me before I ventured out into the first hallway I came to. I went high around the corner, and she went low, but both of our guns barked at the same time.

Our shots resulted in two more faces being irreversibly wrecked as their souls took flight, and that made me smile. The journey was only beginning though, so I kept my composure and focus. We made our way up the hallway and into one of the living rooms on this floor. I knew from studying the pictures that Phillisa had sent me that there were a few blind spots in this house that could exploited, and we were coming up on one fast. I stopped and motioned for Fatz to step up so that we stood three-wide, shoulder-to-shoulder. On my nod, we advanced and hit the corner with bullets already flying. A woman dropped out of the early morning gloom, and the Uzi she'd been holding dropped beside her. I could see two more goons at the end of the hallway, firing at what I assumed were

Phillisa's men, and not paying any attention to us. I motioned towards Mo, and we crept up on them soundlessly. Mo put two bullets in the back of one man's head while I smacked the other one with the butt of my AR.

"Turn over," I demanded, kicking him.

His muttering in Spanish only made me kick him harder because I understood that he was cussing me out.

"Where is Jefe?" I asked.

"Who, puta?"

I put a bullet in his leg for good measure and let him groan in pain.

"I asked you a question, bitch! Where-is-Jefe?" I growled.

"I don't know!" he cried.

"Then you're of no use to me," I said, shooting him with a three-shot burst in the face.

Without a word, I moved on, still following the sounds of multiple guns firing. When I came to a fork in the road I stopped and waited for everyone to catch up. I knew going to the left would result in finding the bedrooms by rounding the corner and going up the stairs. I also knew going to the right would lead to the basement. What I didn't know was where the fuck Campa was in the house, and that was starting to piss me off.

"Split up," I said, pointing for Aubrey, Aaron, Vontrell, and his crew to go towards the bedrooms.

I turned towards the basement, but Mo's hand pulling on my arm stopped me.

"Slow down, Claudette."

I looked at her like she was crazy before pulling my arm away from her and continuing on in the direction I was headed. I came to the basement door and opened it, and as soon as my foot hit the first step, I felt a whoosh of hot air. The ground rumbled beneath my feet as an explosion from the basement lifted the Spanish tiles, along with me, into the air. The way I flew and crashed into the wall behind me knocked the air out of me and made me drop my gun.

The dust and debris in the air was thick enough to blind anyone and it had me choking, while trying to catch my breath. I couldn't see anyone, and my ears were ringing so bad that I couldn't hear whether or not someone was calling me.

"M-Mo!" I yelled, fighting the C-4 fumes clogging my throat.

"Fatz!" I hollered, when I didn't hear Mo respond.

No response from either of them had me struggling to my feet, while using the wall for support. I managed to make it upright, only to have a pair of hands grab me from behind. I felt a quick feeling of relief because one of my people was pulling me out of this wreckage, but when I felt a gloved hand cover my mouth, that relief turned to fear. The moment I started to fight and struggle against my abductor, I felt a heavy smack on the back of my head, and then all I knew was darkness.

When I opened my eyes again, I could see the sun shining brightly all around me, but I was seeing it from my position of being hogtied on the floor of a vehicle. I opened my mouth to scream, before I realized there was a gag taped in place. I tried racking my brain for any way out of this, but I couldn't make my eyes stay open long enough.

There was no way for me to know how long I'd been unconscious again, but when I opened my eyes this time, I could only see darkness. I had no idea where I was, but I knew I wasn't in a car because I could feel that the zip ties around my wrists and ankles were strapped to a chair. It was so dark in the room and I didn't know if I would've been able to see my hand in front of my face. I wasn't sure if my hearing still wasn't back to normal, or I was being held in some sort of soundproof room, but it was deadly quiet. The feeling of grogginess swam through my brain again, but I shook my head vigorously to keep it at bay. I'd never needed to think more than in this moment. I'd been so determined that I'd been sloppy, and that might have cost me and my team their lives. I wouldn't know how bad it was until I knew who actually kidnapped me.

My money was on it being Campa, but I wouldn't put shit past Phillisa at this point. For real, it didn't matter who had kidnapped me, because all that mattered was how the hell I was gonna get out of here. The sudden sound of a key being shoved into a lock made my head snap to the left, even though I still couldn't see. I waited while holding my breath, wondering who would walk through the door.

As the door was slowly pushed open, a light popped on over my head, forcing me to shut my eyes on the sudden brightness. I could feel the involuntary tears leaking from the corners of my eyes, but I still forced them back open so I could face the monster head-on. What I saw made me close my eyes again, because I now knew I was on some type of hallucinogenic. There was no other explanation for what I'd seen, unless I was still unconscious and dreaming.

"There's no need to play sleep, Claudette, I can tell by your breathing that you're fully conscious," Campa said.

I opened my eyes again, wondering if I was trapped inside some type of nightmare I couldn't wake up from.

"Why Claudette, you look like you've seen a ghost," Campa said, chuckling.

I didn't say anything, nor did I take my eyes off of the other man standing beside Campa. His eyes were familiar, but it was obvious that he wasn't the man I used to know.

"I am seeing a ghost because the last time I checked, you were dead, Silk," I said.

"That was a brilliant move on my part, right?" Campa asked, clapping his hands dramatically like a little kid.

"It was definitely a well-played move, and one I never would've given you credit for. It makes sense now though. Of course, you could get to some of my people, and maybe even anticipate some of my moves, when you have the one person I lean on when it's time for war," I said.

"Si. You probably thought I'd eliminated him to make you vulnerable, and that had initially been my plan, until I realized it was too short-sighted. I didn't want you to just be vulnerable, I wanted you right where you are now," he said, smiling wider than any bitch the first time she saw a big black dick.

"Why, Silk?" I asked, trying to hide the hurt I felt behind the anger.

"I didn't have a choice," Silk replied.

"There's always a fucking choice, you bitch-ass nigga!" I growled through clenched teeth.

"Not if he wanted his wife and kids to live through this," Campa said.

I could tell by the way Silk clenched his jaw tightly that Campa was telling the truth. He'd really kidnapped that nigga's family. My thing was that Silk was smart enough to know there was no getting back what he loved the most in this world. Campa wasn't a man to reason with, and he definitely wasn't one you could trust. As absurd as it was, I somehow found myself laughing, and shaking my head in disbelief.

"I'm glad you find this moment amusing, Claudette, because I promise you won't find humor in what comes next."

"I'm not laughing at you, Campa, so check the insecurity you feel about having a small dick. I was laughing at the fact that this dumb ass nigga actually believes you're gonna let him and his family live," I said, smiling at Silk.

"You don't know shit about the deal I made with him, bitch, so shut the fuck up."

"I don't need to know the deal because I know the dealer! It's really common sense though. Do you really think this motherfucker is gonna kidnap the family of a known killer, and then just give them back? Oh, and he's supposed to believe that you're not gonna kill him? Come on, you silly ass nigga, he's gonna kill you and them, just to prevent having to look over his shoulder forever," I said smiling.

Silk was shaking his head in denial, but I could see the light of truth making his eyes shine brighter than the high beams on my truck. It wasn't until Campa pulled out a gun and put it to the back of his head that he was forced to face the truth.

"Did you really not see this coming?" Campa asked.

"You better kill me now, because I promise you won't get another chance," Silk said.

"Oh, don't worry, your death is guaranteed. Just hold on. Marc!" he called out.

A few seconds later, a slim-built, brown-skinned nigga with cornrows came in the room with his gun out. Campa looked at Marc and then nodded towards Silk. Without hesitation, Marc stepped up, and hit Silk hard over the head with his pistol. I watched his eyes go glassy before he fell to the floor at my feet. I took no pleasure in seeing him being dragged from the room, because I knew what was coming to his family. His betrayal had cost them their lives, but it might've ended differently if he would've stayed loyal to me.

"Well, first things first, where's the money you owe me for the coke you stole?"

"Stole? Well, you can't say that I stole from you when you ran away like a little bitch," I replied smiling.

He smiled too, and then swung a vicious hook that landed squarely on my jaw. My head rocked to the left, and I felt something hard shoot down my throat. The taste of blood in my mouth let me know it was one of my teeth I'd swallowed, but I still gave him my best bloody smile. This only made him madder, and he threw two punches to my face. I could feel the blood leaking from my nose, and my eye was already rapidly swelling. Antagonizing him wasn't my smartest course of action, but I knew no other way to stall for time. I doubted that it mattered anyway, but for the sake of my son, I couldn't give up.

"You know, considering that I was your employee, I say we call that coke a severance package. I mean, I think I was unjustly fired, and there is the rather large fact that you killed my husband."

"How much of a husband was he if he fucked my daughter?" he asked, smiling at me.

"Honestly, he was a great husband and father. Maybe if you would've been a better father, your daughter wouldn't have been such a whore."

"Would you say that to her face?" he asked.

"I ain't never been no bitch, and you know that."

He smiled at me, but it never reached his eyes. He looked the part of a reptile that slides on his belly, which was his natural form. It amazed me that it took me so long to see him for who he really was, but I guess this was what happened when you danced with the devil. He pulled his phone out of his pocket and tapped out a quick message while still smiling.

"We'll find out if you're a bitch or not," he said.

I wanted to spit in his face, but before I could work up the phlegm, another figure came around the corner.

"I should've known your trifling ass would double cross me," I said, glaring at Phillisa.

"You should've known because you've gotta answer for the things you've done."

"The things I've done? Oh, you mean killing the child you had with my husband? The child your father knows nothing about?" I asked.

The look Campa turned on her told me the secret I'd just revealed was very much still a secret. This knowledge made me smile.

"You had a baby with that myate? You would disgrace your name, and your body by giving birth to that bastard?" he asked.

"Don't talk about my son like that," she growled.

"He wasn't your son. He was nothing and that's why he died! If you thought having that motherfucker's baby would make him love you, I guess you see how stupid you were. You disgust me, so just kill this bitch so that we can get out of here," he said, waving his hand.

"So, does that mean you don't want the money for the coke, Campa?" I asked.

"I'll have everything that belongs to you in the end anyway. You can die knowing that," he replied.

"What about you, Phillisa? Are you gonna kill me without getting what you want?" I asked.

"You took the only thing in this world I want, bitch, so there's nothing that will save your life," she said, pulling out her gun and pointing it at my head.

"What if I didn't take what you love? What if I told you Asad is still alive, and recovering from his gunshot wound?" I asked, staring straight down the barrel of the Glock .45 in my face.

"You're really gonna lie to try and save your life, you miserable bitch?" she whispered.

I could tell by the way her hand was shaking that she wanted to pull the trigger badly, but the look in her eyes told me that she wanted something else badder. She wanted the hope that I was offering her.

"Shoot her!" Campa insisted.

"He's alive, Phillisa, I can swear to that on Zion Junior's life," I said softly.

"Prove it," she said.

I looked around the room so she would understand that it couldn't happen right here and now.

"I guess I've gotta do it myself, you weakling," Campa said, taking a step forward while raising his pistol.

He never saw the backhand coming, but Phillisa telegraphed it by the slight shift in her shoulders. She smacked Campa squarely in the mouth with the butt of her gun, and he dropped with the speed of an avalanche.

"If you're lying, I'm gonna kill your son after I kill you," she said, tucking her gun in her pants as she moved behind me.

Within seconds, I felt the restraints fall away from my ankles and wrists. I stood up and turned to face her, preparing to reassure her, but what I saw stopped me cold.

"Wh-where did you get that?" I asked, nodding at the pearl-handled straight razor in her hand.

She looked at it like this was her first time seeing it, and then her eyes met mine.

"I've had it for years, now where is my son?"

"I didn't ask you how long you had it…I asked where you got it?" I repeated.

"It was Zion's."

Chapter 14

"I know that's Zion's. And I know he had it the night he died. What I don't know is how you came to have it in your possession," I said, taking a step towards her.

Her gun came back up swiftly, levelled in my direction.

"That's not important, Claudette, because you need to worry about proving that my son is alive. And you need to do it right now if you ever hope to step out of this room alive," she said, digging her phone out of her pocket, and passing it to me.

I stared hard at her for a moment, before taking the phone from her hand. I instinctively wanted to call Mo to find out if she made it out of the house alive, but the look in Phillisa's eyes spoke of how little patience she had. Plus, we absolutely needed to get out of Dodge before Campa came to, or his men came calling. I dialed Meatrock's number and listened to it ring twice.

"Who is this?" he asked suspiciously.

"It's me."

"Cl-Claudette, is it really you?" he asked, close to tears.

"Give me the damn phone," Mo said immediately.

I heard some brief rustling, and then Mo's voice.

"This better not be a fucking joke. Is this really you, Snow?"

"It's me, but I don't have much time," I replied, looking at Phillisa.

"Put the phone on speaker," Phillisa said.

I did as I was told, but I really wanted to knock this bitch out.

"Where are you?" Mo asked.

"That's irrelevant. You need to send me proof of life," Phillisa said impatiently.

"Proof of life? Bitch, I'm gonna bury you!" Mo yelled.

"Not if I bury you first, hoe. Now where the fuck is my son?"

"What son?" Mo asked innocently.

The sound of Phillisa pulling the slide back on the pistol, and chambering a round, was loud enough for Mo to hear. I knew she heard it because she cussed loudly.

"Hold on, bitch," Mo said, sucking her teeth.

We could hear her moving, and Meatrock asking a million questions as she walked away from him.

"Watch out, Doc, I need to take a quick picture," Mo said.

I didn't hear Kevin's response, but I could see the look of unchecked hope flood Phillisa's eyes. A few moments later, the phone vibrated in my hand, and I passed it to Phillisa. I had no idea what condition Asad was in, but whatever Phillisa saw had her in tears instantly.

"Y-you didn't kill him," she whispered.

"No, but your father tried to. If he knew he was still alive, he'd try again and you know it, but this is who you chose to align yourself with."

"Give Asad to me," she said, looking up from the picture at me.

"Give Campa to me," I countered.

The indecision I saw in her eyes made me wonder how deep her daddy issues ran. It wasn't until she looked over my shoulder past me that I understood her hesitation was about our escape.

"Are your men out there?" I asked.

"Yeah, but—"

"You're outnumbered, right?"

The look she gave me said it all.

"Where are you?" Mo asked.

"There's no time for you to get here, so we'll have to do this ourselves. Where are you?" Phillisa countered.

"You don't need to know that. All you need to know is that you'll get your son back if we make it out of here alive," I said.

I could tell by the way she looked at me that she really didn't like what I was saying, but we'd have to agree to disagree for now. Her son was the only thing keeping me alive, and I'd be an idiot to give up my leverage.

"We'll contact you when we're back in the states," Phillisa said, hanging up on Mo.

"I hope you have a plan," I said.

"Maybe, but it doesn't involve me giving you a weapon, so that you can kill me when I'm not looking."

I smiled so I wouldn't have to deny the truth in her statement.

"Turn around," she demanded.
"For what?"
"Because we have to set the stage to make this shit believable," she replied.

I was hesitant to comply, but the reality was that this was her show and I was just a role player. I turned around and put my hands behind my back, expecting some more zip ties to grace my wrists. I wasn't expecting to find myself suddenly falling on my face from a blow to the back of the head. My vision swam, but I was still able to see her step over my body and walk out of the room.

Everything in me wanted to get up off the floor, but I could only lay there. I could feel the blood leaking from my head running down the side of her face, and it only served to make me madder. I could hear the sound of voices, and then the sound of footsteps rapidly approaching. I closed my eyes and waited for the cavalry.

"She got the drop on him, but I fixed that ass real quick," Phillisa said.

"Did you kill her?"

"Probably, but just in case, I want you two to carry her out to my truck. You two carry my father and put him in the passenger seat of my truck so I can take him home," she replied.

"But I thought your father wanted—"

"Are you really about to tell me what my father wants?" she asked aggressively.

"N-no."

"I didn't think so. Move," she demanded.

A few seconds later, I felt myself being lifted into the air, and I had to remind myself to go limp. The strong hands carrying me were frisky as shit though because they were conveniently grabbing my titties and ass. If my life didn't depend on me being unconscious, I would've snapped the fuck out, but I played my position. I was thrown across a seat, and I didn't stop sliding until my head hit the door. I bit my tongue to avoid crying out, but I damn near blacked out. A few moments later, the truck started and we were moving.

"Can you hear me, Claudette?"

"Fuck you, bitch," I slurred.

"Just keep your head down and try not to move too much."

I wanted to keep cussing her out, but something more important came out of my mouth. I barely got to hang my head off of the seat before the vomit shot out of my nose, and mouth.

"What the fuck?" Phillisa exclaimed.

"F-fuck you," I said, laying my head back on the seat.

I didn't know how long we rode for, but the sudden stop made my stomach lurch again. I fought the bile back, but just barely.

"You're gonna have to walk, Snow, there's no one here to help us," she said, opening the door.

She had to halfway drag me out of the truck and lean me up against it. The smell of salt water filled my nose and made me open my eyes. What I saw was a big beautiful white yacht with a lion on the back.

"Travelling in style, I see," I said, shaking my head slowly in hopes of clearing some of the fogginess away.

Phillisa threw one of my arms over her shoulder, and we walked slowly down the dock to the waiting boat. Once we got onboard, she sat me down in the first chair we came to, and then she disappeared out of sight. She was back a few minutes later with a still unconscious Campa, and she sat him next to me. The boats engine's roared to life, and moments later we were moving out into the open waters. I should've felt relief, but I didn't because I was smart enough to know that I wasn't home free yet.

"I think you fractured my skull, bitch," I said, gingerly touching my head.

"You'll live, and you're welcome by the way," she replied, digging zip ties out of her pocket, and using them to restrain Campa.

"Don't act like you saved me out of the kindness of your heart bitch. You did it to save your son."

"And you better keep your end of this deal, or you'll know what's worse than death," she vowed, looking over at me.

I didn't say anything, and she finished up securing Campa. He started to move around and shake his head like he was trying to come out of the darkness, but she quickly pulled her pistol back out and smacked him again.

"Don't kill him, I want that pleasure," I said seriously.

She left him slumped on the lounge chair and stepped back over to me.

"Come on, let's get you cleaned up."

I looked at her warily, but I still accepted the help she offered and stood up. By the time we made it downstairs into one of the cabins I was out of breath.

"Why the fuck do I feel so weak?" I asked.

"You've been doped up for days, and not moving around."

"Days? What the fuck are you talking about?" I asked, looking at her closely.

"I know it must've only felt like a day or two at the most, but you were out for five days. That was how you were constantly moved around Cuba, because trust me when I tell you your people turned over every rock. If it wasn't for the political influence Campa had bought, we probably would've still been moving around. He was able to force your people to retreat and leave the country, or they would've become political prisoners."

None of this information should've surprised me, but it did, and it made me want to kill Campa even more.

"If I would've known Asad was...that you didn't hurt him—"

"You would've come to my rescue sooner?" I asked sarcastically.

"I wasn't lying to you when I told you I wasn't a part of the initial attack against you. The only reason I went to see that bastard to begin with, is because I didn't want him to hurt you."

"Oh, so you were trying to save me? That was mighty white of you," I replied in the same sarcastic tone.

I could tell she wanted to keep talking to try and convince me of her sincerity, but she thought better of it. She helped me into the bathroom and left me leaning up against the Jacuzzi tub. I struggled to get my clothes off, and when I caught a whiff of my body's odor, I believed what she'd said about me being out for days. I'd apparently started my period in the process too, which sucked and swallowed. My limbs felt sore, which I attributed to lack of voluntary use. I fought through the discomfort and got into the tub, where I turned on the water and waited, I had the tub halfway full before Phillisa reappeared with a washcloth and towel. She sat them on the corner of the sink, and then came towards me.

"Are you okay?" she asked.

"Even when I'm not."

"I'm just gonna check your head real quick," she said, grabbing the washcloth and stepping behind me.

I flinched involuntarily, but I didn't say anything when I felt her fingers gently parting my hair.

"This is gonna burn a little," she said, reaching for a bar of soap sitting on the side of the tub.

When she unwrapped it, the fragrance of jasmine wafted through the air, and it had an oddly calming effect on me. I sat still with my eyes closed as she cleaned my wound, wishing it was that easy to clean everything else that ached within me. When I suddenly felt her hand moving the washcloth across my collarbone, I tensed up, but I didn't open my eyes or say anything. I was afraid to say anything because I had no idea of what I would say. Her movements were slow and methodical, but also shy and curious.

"Scoot forward a little," she said softly.

I did as she requested, and when I felt her climb into the tub with me, I finally opened my eyes. I didn't turn around to look at her, and the question of whether she had clothes on was answered when I felt the heat of her flesh pressed against my back. She pulled me back towards her so that I was half-laying, half-sitting in her lap. She continued washing me gently, taking one breast in her hand at a time and caressing me with a familiarity I wished she didn't have. I could feel my body betraying me as my nipples got hard, and the pain in between my legs was replaced by a throbbing desire. When she started working her way down my stomach with the washcloth, I caught her hand and stopped her.

"We can't do this, Phillisa."

"Why not? I know you want to, and in your heart, you know I never wanted to kill you," she replied, kissing my neck softly.

"I also know you had an ongoing affair with Zion too."

My words froze her actions, and I felt her lean backwards away from me.

"What do you want me to say, Claudette? What happened with Zion was wrong, and I won't act like it wasn't. What happened between you and I wasn't though. I fell in love with Claudette Snow, not Mrs. Zion Snow."

"They're the same person, and that's what you don't understand," I said, shaking my head.

"But you know what I do understand? I understand that before you knew anything, you were falling in love with me. I understand that you still love me now, but you're fighting it with everything in you. Why?" she asked.

"Because I can't get past the fact that your affair cost me my husband, and my son his father. Do you understand that?"

My question left her silent, but she didn't get up and leave. I felt a slight tug of something inside me because her son had lost his father too. We both knew she wasn't shit for fucking a married man, but Asad was innocent in all of this. I had to remember that.

"Look, I understand that Asad lost his father too, and I...I know it must be hard on you, knowing your actions contributed to that. I'm not insensitive to the guilt you carry, I'm just not about to carry it with you," I said.

"You don't have to carry any guilt, Claudette. I mean, do you really think Zion expected you to be a saint for the rest of your life?"

"Probably not, but he also didn't expect me to fuck his mistress either," I replied.

In her silence this time, I heard her understanding, so I knew I didn't have to repeat myself again. I did have an idea though, and once it had spun the block in my mind, I knew it was the right move.

"You can finish bathing me though, since you did give me a concussion," I said, laying back against her.

She chuckled softly, but she did pick up the washcloth, and went back to work. The sexual tension was thick, but I fought the urge to fuck her or get fucked. I could tell with every move of the rag in her hand that she was trying to seduce me, but I wouldn't make it that easy for her.

Aryanna

When my fingers were wrinkled, I stopped her hand from moving over my body, and told her I was ready to get out. She got up and helped me out of the tub so I could go to my room. I hadn't expected her to follow me, but I should've known she wouldn't give up that easy. She came into my room, dried me off from head to toe, and then rubbed lotion into my skin until I had goose bumps from her touch.

"You're not getting any pussy," I said.

"That's what you say now, but I know you're wet as shit." I wanted to smack the smirk off her damn face, but instead I let her have her moment.

"I might let you get some after Campa is dead. We could celebrate that way."

"If that's all it takes, then we can kill his ass now," she said.

I was waiting on her to laugh, but she didn't. I got dressed without her help, and then I put my plan into motion.

"Did you really mean what you said?" I asked.

"What are you talking about?"

"I'm talking about you being in love with me," I said, looking at her closely.

"I wouldn't have said it if I didn't mean it, Snow."

"Well, when this is all over, we can have a different conversation. Right now though, we need to focus on the goals we have in mind," I said.

She nodded at me, and I could see the smile pulling at her lips.

"Now that that's settled, what do you have to eat in this motherfucker?" I asked.

"I'll feed you, baby. I'll always have something for you to eat."

Chapter 15

Three Days Later

"Mom!" Junior screamed, running into my arms and knocking me down into the snow.

I laughed while hugging him tightly and letting out the tears of joy I felt.

"You're too big to be running up on me like that," I said.

"I've missed you sooooo much though, Mom. Where have you been?"

"I had some business out of the country, but I'm here now. I missed you too, and I'm sorry I haven't been around much," I replied.

He didn't say anything, but he didn't have to, because I knew my son. I had no idea what he'd been told when everyone thought I was dead, but it was obvious that he'd felt something was off. I had no doubt that my life force was connected to his because he was what I lived for. The flip side of that was that he got intuitive feelings, and I knew he'd been able to feel that something was wrong.

"Junior, let your mom up out of that snow before she freezes to death," Mo said, walking over to us.

"Our last name is Snow, which means we'll be okay," he replied, laughing giddily.

Mo caught us both by surprise when she picked him up by his jacket and airlifted him off of me. He was laughing of course, and that warmed me from head to toe. I got up faster than I had in days, but no sooner had I reached my feet when Mo was on me, knocking me back into the snow.

"Now bitch, you know better," I said, laughing hard.

"Shut up, I missed you too," she said, kissing me quickly on the lips.

"No fair!" Junior said, jumping on Mo's back.

We were all laughing so hard that we didn't pay attention to the sound of the horn being honked until it became insistent. I could see the flash of hatred swim fast into Mo's eyes, but I knew she would keep it cute for now.

"Hop up, Junior," I said.

Once he got up, Mo followed his lead, and she pulled me up with her. I looked back at the Suburban, and even though I couldn't see through the tint, I could feel Phillisa's eyes on me. I could feel her jealousy like it was heat, melting the snow around us.

"So, how is this gonna go?" Mo asked, moving closer to me so Junior wouldn't overhear us.

"I'm playing it by ear, but I've got an end game. I need you to trust me though."

I looked at her when I spoke these words, and I immediately spotted her desire to yell, "Hell no," at me.

"I trust you…I don't trust the people around you," she said.

"I don't expect you to trust anyone except Anastasia."

My use of her God-given name made her smile and shake her head.

"Why can't we just deal with her once we have her in the house?" Mo asked.

"Because she's smarter than that. That's why she wanted to meet with you in person before we went to the house."

"I don't understand," she said, clearly confused.

"You will," I said, motioning for Phillisa to get out of the truck. When her feet hit the snow, I felt Mo's temperature rise instantly.

"Junior, I want you to get back in the truck, and we're gonna follow you back to the house," I said.

"But I wanna go with you, Mom."

"I'm not going anywhere, I promise, but we need to have an adult conversation so please get in the truck," I said.

I could tell he wanted to argue based on the frown riding his features, but he didn't wanna piss me off. Phillisa waited until he was back in the truck before she approached us.

"You're a bold bitch, I'll give you that," Mo said.

"You're not giving it to me, I'm taking it," she replied, smiling.

I put a quick hand on Mo's chest to stop her from advancing on Phillisa.

"Don't," I said.

"Why the fuck not?" Mo growled angrily.

Before I could respond, Phillisa opened her jacket and lifted her shirt up.

"Is that—"

"Yeah, that's C-4 and yeah, it's strapped to my body. It's connected to a dead switch, so if I die or stop breathing, then so does everyone in a four-block radius," Phillisa said.

The self-satisfied smug smile on her face made me want to shoot her my damn self, but I resisted. At least for now.

"You're smarter than I gave you credit for," Mo said sarcastically.

"That's obvious, so let's just cut the shit and get down to it. I've made a deal with Snow, and as you can see, I kept my part of it. So now, I want my son, and we'll consider this an official truce," Phillisa said.

"Sure thing, but you should probably know I'm gonna kill you at some point in this life. You don't get to just walk away from the bodies you've dropped," Mo replied smiling.

"I look forward to you trying, bitch."

I could feel it in my soul, this shit was about to get out of hand, so I cut their exchange short by pushing Phillisa back towards our truck.

"We'll follow you, Mo," I called over my shoulder.

I waited until we were back in the Suburban before I said anything to Phillisa. "Why you gotta be so extra all the damn time, bitch?"

"Because I don't like that hoe, and you know that," she replied.

"I didn't realize that was the reason you were freezing your ass off in Colorado. Stay focused, Phillisa."

I started the truck, and pulled off behind Mo. It took us an hour to get up the mountain to the house, and we didn't exchange a single word the entire time. When we stopped in the driveway, the front door opened, and Meatrock stepped out with a custom-made chrome AR-15. The look on his face was neutral, but the gun looked angry as fuck!

Aryanna

"You might wanna get out and make the announcement that no one can shoot me, or otherwise harm me in any way," she said, looking over at me.

"No need."

As she'd been talking, Mo had gotten out to have a word with Meatrock. When his eyes swung towards our truck, I knew Mo had told him what was going on. To say he was unhappy was an understatement, because I could see the fire in his eyes reflecting off the snow. I gave him a few seconds to gather his composure, and then I got out. I walked over to him and pulled him into my arms.

"It's gonna be alright, trust me," I whispered in his ear.

"She's gotta die, Snow."

"Trust me, Antonio," I repeated, pulling back to look him in the eyes.

He nodded reluctantly, and I turned around to summon Phillisa. She got out the truck and strolled over to where we stood. Without a word Mo turned and went in the house, summoning Junior to follow her. I waved at him because I could tell by his hesitation that he wanted to come over to me.

"Where's Asad?" Phillisa asked impatiently.

"Safe, in the house," Meatrock replied, staring hard at her.

"Lead the way," she said to me.

"Just go on in, and we'll handle the business out here," I replied.

"Nice try, Claudette, but you know damn well I'm not walking through that door without you glued to my hip."

"You scared?" Meatrock asked.

"I ain't scared of shit, nigga." I chuckled softly because I could tell the question offended her deeply.

I could also tell she was scared on some level, but that could've been about her son.

"Come on. I'll send somebody back out here in a minute," I said, leading the way in the house.

As soon as I came through the door, I was lifted off of my feet by Aubrey, and bear hugged.

"I'm glad you've got nine lives," he said.

"More like eighteen lives," Aaron said, coming over to me.

140

I was passed from one brother to another without my feet ever touching the ground.

"I'm glad you guys made it out of there alive," I said, fighting to keep my emotions in check.

"No thanks to the bitch behind you, but it takes more than a clever plan to kill us," Aubrey said.

"Ain't that the truth," a female's voice said.

I looked over Aaron's shoulder, and my mouth fell open.

"L-Lexx? How the fuck are you alive? Where's Ashlee?" I asked, looking around.

No one spoke or made eye contact with me, and that was all the answer I needed. I tapped Aaron so he'd put me down, and I went straight into Alexas' arms. She held onto me tightly, and I could feel her tears sliding down my neck.

"It's okay, sweetie, you're here and you're safe," I murmured.

When she got herself together, she pulled back so she could look up at me.

"I was under the house exploring the caves, because-because I thought they were cool. Ashlee was upstairs. I couldn't hear anything really, but I felt the ground shake so hard that I chipped a tooth," she said.

"I saw the house and there's no way you would've survived if you had been upstairs," I said.

"I know," she whispered.

I could see the guilt taking laps in the infinity pools that were her eyes. I couldn't carry that burden for her, but I knew how to help ease it a little.

"The motherfucker responsible is outside in the back of my rental truck," I said.

I didn't have to say shit else because Aaron and Aubrey were out the door.

"Uh, before you get to that, I'd like to see my son," Phillisa said.

The tension immediately ratcheted up a notch, but Junior defused it just as quick.

"Are you my little brother's mom?"

"I-I am," Phillisa said, looking at me.

"Oh. Well, he's sleeping, but I'll take you to him," Junior offered.

I nodded my head at her to let her know it was okay, and she followed Junior down the hallway.

"Does she really have a bomb strapped to her?" Lexx whispered.

"She does, and it has a kill switch, along with a manual detonation switch," I replied.

I could see the disappointment written all over Lexx's face, and I could hear it in the deep breaths taken by everyone around me.

"I promise you all, everything is gonna be alright," I said reassuringly.

"You better be right, because we've got more trouble to deal with," Mo said.

"What now?" I asked.

"Campa's people know he's missing, and they've made an educated guess about you being involved," Mo stated.

"That's not surprising, given how things unfolded. I've got a plan," I said.

"Does that plan somehow involve getting more coke, because your supply is limited," Mo said.

I cursed softly under my breath while shaking my head. One of the things I'd forgotten was that I still had a business to run.

"Where's Fatz?" I asked.

"He's out with Alexia right now, but he'll be back soon," Lexx said.

"Alright listen, I want you all to pack up the house and get ready to leave," I said.

"Where are we going?" Meatrock asked.

I looked at Mo and considered where a nice location would be to keep everyone safe.

"I say a spot where you have no nosy neighbors, and no traffic. A place like that is hard to sneak up to," Mo said.

"Sounds like the middle of nowhere," Lexx said.

"That's the idea, and I know just the place, so start packing," I replied smiling.

The sound of the door opening had our eyes moving in that direction, and Meatrock bringing the AR-15 up to a firing position. It was only Aubrey and Aaron though, carrying an unconscious Campa.

"Put him in one of the bedrooms until the kids are gone," I said.

"So how are we gonna handle all of this, Snow?" Mo asked.

All eyes were on me now, but I didn't feel any pressure. I felt the power I'd earned.

"The first thing that we need to do is replenish our army. Mo, I want you to reach out to Silk's brother, Duke, and tell him we need him. He'll ride on the nigga who killed Silk. I'll reach out to Nicki's twin sister, JoJo, and have the same talk with her," I said.

"Nicki has a twin?" Meatrock asked.

"I'm gonna need you to act like BeBe is in the other room with your kids, my nigga," I replied, shaking my head.

The blush that lit up his face made it clear where his mind had been, but I didn't talk funky to him like I could've.

"Mo, let me holla at you real quick. Everybody else, start packing," I said.

When everyone started moving, I led Mo back outside so we could talk in private.

"What's wrong, Snow?"

"You need to know about Silk. He was helping Campa, and that's why it seemed like we could never get ahead. He kidnapped Silk's family and made him go against us in order to get them back."

"Silk had to know his family was almost certainly dead either way, so why would he—"

"Because hope is a powerful and dangerous narcotic. Silk learned the hard way though, because the last time I saw him was when Campa put a gun to his head and had him taken away. So, either way, he's dead now and we'll use his brother to go against Campa's people," I said.

"Okay. I'm assuming that you want this to stay between you and I."

"Yeah, because the less his brother knows, the better. I also need to let you know I'm about to use Phillisa to get our supply back up. Before you say anything, just hear me out. She can't cross us again because by now, Campa's people know she helped me escape, and kidnapped or killed him. There's no going back for her. My plan is still to destroy that bitch by any means necessary, and I put that on Zion. I'm just gonna take her for everything she has first," I said.

"Claudette, you better know what you're doing."

"I do, bitch, I do," I replied, pulling her towards me and hugging her.

"Alright now, I need you to go help everybody get their shit together because the relocation spot will be Vegas."

"Vegas? Why Vegas?" she asked, confused.

"Because there's a lot of desert space out there, and you can see a motherfucker coming from a long way off."

"Makes sense, I guess. Do you need me to make the arrangements?" she asked.

"Yeah."

She nodded her head before turning and going back inside. I took a few minutes to make a couple necessary phone calls, and then I went back inside, to find Aubrey waiting on me.

"What are we gonna do with him?" he asked.

"What do you wanna do?"

"There's a fire pit out back," he replied.

"I'll get the marshmallows," I said smiling.

He smiled too before heading back up the hallway. I took a deep breath, and then headed to the room Asad was in.

"How's he doing, Kevin?" I asked, pausing outside his door.

"He's a strong and courageous little boy, and I've never seen anything like him, honestly."

"That doesn't surprise me. His dad was a hell of a man, and his mother is a force of nature," I said.

"I kinda got that feeling when she stormed in the room and demanded I get out."

"I'm sorry about that. I do wanna tell you we will be leaving here soon, so where do you want your money sent to?" I asked.

"You really don't have to pay me any—"

"Kevin, we had an agreement, so there's no use arguing."

"Okay, okay. I'll give you my bank information, and you can do whatever you want from there," he said.

I pulled out my phone and passed it to him. Once he was done locking his info in, he passed it back, and I went into Asad's room. I didn't know if they'd been talking about me, but all conversation ceased when I came in, and their eyes swung in my direction.

"Th-that's her, Mom," he said softly.

"I'm who?" I asked.

"He said an angel saved him. That he could feel her carrying him, and he felt safe even though he was hurt," she said, looking at me with tears in her eyes.

"I'm not an angel, Asad, I'm just someone who cares about you," I replied.

"My brother says you're an angel, but you're a gangster too," he said, matter-of-factly.

This statement got a smile out of Phillisa and me.

"Can I borrow your mom for a minute, Asad?"

"As long as she keeps her promise."

"Promise?" I asked, looking Phillisa in the eyes.

"She promised to always come back to me," he said.

I nodded my head in understanding, and then I motioned for her to follow me out. Once we were in the hallway, I sent Kevin back in to make sure Asad was okay, and ready to travel.

"I'm moving everyone," I said.

"I'm taking my son with me, Claudette, that was our deal."

"That was before Campa's people were hurting both of us. You know like I do, being anywhere near you right now is a death sentence for that little boy. The same goes for my son, so don't think I don't feel your pain. The reality is that this war ain't over and until it is, no one is safe. So, it's your choice. Do you wanna raise your son or mourn him?" I asked.

The tears that popped up in her eyes were anger, and I knew this because I knew she'd mourned her son once. She'd rather die than do that again.

"Tell me you've got a plan, bitch."

Aryanna

"Of course I do, but first things first. Your father dies," I replied.

Chapter 16

"There's no need to play sleep, Campa, I can tell by your breathing that you're fully conscious," I said smiling.

When he still refused to open his eyes, I gave Aubrey the nod, and he brought his steel-toed Timberland down on Campa's face. The sound of bones crushing was music to my ears, and the scream that followed the crushing was like having my favorite song on repeat.

"Nice of you to join us, Jefe. Now, I'm not a cold-hearted woman, so I'll give you this moment to say your last words. I'm sure you never gave Zion that courtesy, and I know you didn't give it to Tony," I said.

When he opened his mouth to speak, Aaron stepped forward and put a boot to his face again.

"He didn't give Ashlee that chance," Aaron said.

When Campa screamed this time, two of his teeth fell out of his mouth, and that made my smile widen.

"Cl-Claudette..."

Before he could get past my name, Phillisa stepped up, and kicked him in the face harder than anyone had.

"You almost killed my son!" she raged.

I could tell Campa was on the verge of losing consciousness again, which meant it was time to get this over with.

"Put him in the pit, Fatz," I ordered.

Fatz quickly scooped him up out of the bloody snow and dumped his still-bound body into the fire pit. While Aaron poured a mixture of gas and kerosene all over Campa, Mo went around the circle we'd formed around him passing each of us a stick. On the end of each stick were two marshmallows. Mo held my stick so I could light the book of matches in my hand.

"It's been real, Campa. See you on the other side," I said, dropping the matches on his face.

His whole body burst into flames faster than dominoes falling, and suddenly there was a raging bonfire lighting up the evening sky. While he screamed and pleaded for the pain to stop, we all stood around him watching, and roasting marshmallows joyfully. Even after he stopped screaming, I poured more of the accelerant on his charred remains and watched as the fire grew again.

"Well, now that that's done, what's the next move?" Phillisa asked.

"Are you sure you don't want to say a few words about your amazing daddy?" Mo asked sarcastically.

"You know what, bitch—"

"Ay, we're not about to do this shit, so both of you shut the fuck up," I said.

I could tell Mo didn't like how I talked to her, but I had no patience for the dumb shit.

"We're about to go back to Florida, and right now that's the equivalent of stepping into a live warzone. We need to mentally prepare for that. We've got a shipment of coke coming in tomorrow morning, courtesy of our new supplier, and we need to flood the streets immediately. Fatz, I want you to get with Gunz and J5 on that, and I want that dope to flow. I checked with some people, and the Columbians are definitely in town looking for anyone connected to me. So, we're coming in hot, and we're gonna lay shit down like our livelihood depends on it. Understand?" I asked.

Everyone nodded their head, and I could see the look of determination in their eyes.

"Are Chyna and Lexx supposed to join us in Florida?" Aaron asked.

"Nah, I want as much protection around those kids as possible, and I want people I can trust. Meatrock is meeting us in Florida though," I replied.

I could see the relief in Phillisa's eyes when I stated my goal of keeping the kids safe. I didn't know if she expected me to hate her son because he was a product of my husband's infidelity, but she was way off. We all stood there and watched Campa burn, until there was nothing left of him but a memory.

"Alright, let's get going," I said, finishing off my last marshmallow.

We loaded up the trucks and headed down the mountain. It took us about an hour and a half to get to the airport, but the plane was fueled and waiting, so we were able to take to the sky immediately. Once we were up amongst the clouds, Mo summoned me to the office on the plane for a strategy discussion.

"I know you've got a plan for when the dust settles but tell me you're not really about to trust this bitch to play it straight, Snow."

"Do I look like Boo-Boo the damn fool? You know that I'm smarter than that, and you also know she serves a purpose right now. Having the Columbians on our ass ain't no little thing, because that nigga I just killed was kinda like a big deal. So, aligning ourselves with the power on her side of the cartel, increases our chances of staying alive," I replied.

"All of that sounds good, but I remember how quickly she had you under her spell the last time."

"Ah, so you're worried about us fucking! I mean, it was you who accused me of being pussy whipped, right?" I asked sarcastically.

"Snow, I don't wanna fight with you, and you're grown so I can't tell you who to fuck. I'm just gonna make a suggestion though. Her pussy is dangerous, and the fact that your husband ain't here should be all the evidence you need."

Without waiting for my response, she turned around and walked out of the room. I took a seat in one of the chairs in the room and tried to recover from the verbal shotgun I'd just taken to the face. Before I could put my mind back on business though, the door opened again and Phillisa stepped in.

"Were your ears burning?" I asked, shaking my head at her timing.

"No, but it doesn't surprise me that my good friend Mo would have something negative to say. I could probably guess how your conversation went, but I honestly couldn't care less. All I care about is coming out of this alive. Are we on the same page?"

"We are. In the meantime, I need you to try and get along with Mo, because if she should catch an accidental bullet I'm gonna blame you," I replied seriously.

Aryanna

"I hear you loud and clear. Are we gonna have the conversation about you and me?"

"Now is soooo not the time for that shit, so I'll pass," I said.

"Okay. I just thought I'd bring it up while we have a little privacy."

I was sorely tempted to shoot the smile off of her face, but she vanished back out the door first. I took the moment alone to FaceTime with the kids, and make sure they were adjusting to the desert heat. Of course, Junior wouldn't let me off the phone until I agreed to come out there, sooner than later. I knew his understanding for my business only went so far, so I promised to see him soon, and he promised to look after his brother. Kevin had recommended an amazing travel nurse, and she'd linked up with Alexas in Vegas. Still, I knew Asad had to be scared, so having Junior around him was more than helpful.

After that call, I hit up Red Gunz and told him we'd be landing in about two and a half hours, and I wanted nothing short of a motorcade to meet us on the tarmac. Our destination was one of the houses that Mo had had the good sense to purchase. It had been fortified like my old house use to be, and I felt like our safety would be secured. With that taken care of I turned my attention to finding the whereabouts of those who were in town looking for me.

"When was the last time you ate something?" Mo asked, sitting a plate in front of me with a sandwich on it.

"Honestly, other than those marshmallows I couldn't tell you. Things are beyond crazy right now."

"Yeah, they are, but that doesn't mean you get to neglect yourself. So, eat," she said, pushing the plate towards me.

I put my phone down, picked up the hoagie, and took a healthy bite. While I chewed the lettuce, turkey, cheese, and mayonnaise I watched Mo closely. Her eyes stayed locked on mine, and that told me she definitely had some shit on her mind.

"What's up, Anastasia?"

"What do you mean?" she asked.

"I mean, it's obvious you've got something on your mind, so just spit it out."

"I can't really put it into words. I've just got a bad feeling, Claudette."

I contemplated her words for a moment, and then did a mental evaluation to see if what she was saying matched anything inside myself. I'd been taught to listen to and trust my instincts, and I also trusted the instincts of those around me.

"What's causing these feelings?" I asked.

"I don't know. At first, I thought it was just Phillisa, but I think it's deeper than that. Like…like we're walking into something we can't see or prepare for."

"In a sense we are, because we have only limited info about what's been going on recently. There's nothing we can't handle though," I said.

"Snow, you got a second?" Phillisa asked, from the doorway.

"Except her," Mo mumbled, before turning and moving past Phillisa.

"Now what?" I asked impatiently.

She stepped all the way into the room, stopped in front of me and tossed a pearl-handled straight razor on the desk, Zion's razor. I looked up at her and waited for her to speak, but I didn't pick the razor up.

"The night Zion died… I was there. I felt him take his last breath, and I watched as the light left his eyes. That's how I got this razor, because he put it in my hands himself. I should've given it to you then, but I couldn't look you in the face. At the time, I blamed myself for not watching his back better, but now I blame myself for different reasons. He wanted you to have it though, and I'm sorry I didn't give it to you sooner," she said.

My eyes were locked on hers, but I still didn't speak. I didn't know what I was supposed to say to her revelation, but the anger building in my chest told me it wasn't gonna be nice. Eventually, she got that feeling though, because she simply turned around, and left the room. I continued eating my sandwich, but now my eyes were fixated on the razor. I was seeing its pretty pearl handle catching the light from the chandelier, as Zion cut my Gucci dress open.

I could see the smile on his face as he kissed me, and it made my pussy throb.

Suddenly, I could see what was left of him lying on the cold slab of the coroner's table. The throbbing quickly moved from my pussy to my heart, forcing me to put my food down and fight to catch my breath. It took me a few minutes to regain my composure and when I did, I realized the pearl handle was grasped firmly in my grip. To feel like I was drawing power from it seemed ridiculous, but I knew it was happening, nonetheless.

I closed my eyes and sat there holding the razor, until the captain came over the loudspeaker and announced our imminent landing. When I opened my eyes and tucked the razor in my bra, I knew there was only one word to describe my intentions. Murderous. I got up and went back out to take my seat, and strap in. I could feel Phillisa's eyes on me, but I directed my attention to Mo.

"When we land, I want everybody to go to the house, but you're coming with me," I said.

"I got you," Mo replied.

"Wait, hold up, I'm going too," Phillisa said.

"No, you're going to the house until I tell you what the plan is," I stated forcefully.

Everything in her body wanted to argue with me, and Mo had the look in her eyes that said if she opened her mouth again, shit would get ugly. Phillisa was definitely smart enough to read the tea leaves, so she ain't say shit. We landed, and when I stepped off the plane, we were surrounded by five black 2022 Expeditions, and one of my Lamborghini's.

"Fatz, get everybody settled in, and wait for my call," I said, walking down the stairs and going to my car.

When Red Gunz stepped out of my car, he passed me a chrome and black Glock .27.

"I'll meet you back at the house. Send one truck with me and Mo, and you all go with everybody else to the house," I said.

"I got you," he replied.

I slid behind the wheel and waited on Mo to climb in beside me. As soon as her ass hit the seat, I put the car in gear, and pulled off fast.

"Where are we going, Snow?"

"To pay a visit to the one person in Miami that knows everything about everybody." I replied.

She didn't speak for a moment, but then I saw her smile out of the corner of my eye.

"The bag man?" she asked.

"The bag man."

"And you actually think he's gonna answer your questions?" she asked.

"I know he is."

She didn't question me any further and an hour later, we were creeping through a suburban, tree-lined, rich neighborhood. I parked the car about a block from the destination, and we got out. The bag man was actually a nigga named King Devine, and he had his fingers on the pulse of the streets. He knew more than where the bodies were buried, and that's what pretty much made him untouchable. His problem was that I didn't give a damn who said he couldn't be touched.

"What's our play to get inside?" Mo asked.

"You're gonna go ring the doorbell."

I could feel her eyes burning a hole in the side of my head through the darkness surrounding us, but I ignored it.

"Seriously, Snow, how are we getting in?"

I stopped and faced her while digging in my pocket. I pulled out a zip tie and held it out to her.

"Put this around my wrists in the front, put your gun in my side, and ring the doorbell. I'd bet my left tittie there's a bounty on me, and it's huge. Therefore, a man like King Devine won't be able to ignore it, or the gift you're bringing to his doorstep. Once we're inside, we play it by ear until we have what we came for."

She was shaking her head like she didn't like the plan, but she was already tightening the zip ties around my outstretched wrists.

"Are you ready?" she asked.

"Absolutely."

We headed in the direction of the house King Devine and his family stayed in, making sure to keep our eyes open. I knew the security here had to be top of the line, which meant that he knew the moment we'd stepped on his property. My theory was proven true when Mo knocked on the door, and it was opened less than ten seconds later.

"Are you crazy?" he said in a furious whisper.

"Obviously. Now, are you gonna ask dumb ass questions all night, or get us out of plain sight?" Mo asked.

"Y-you can't just bring a bound woman to my fucking front steps! That's not how this works, Morano."

"Oh, so you don't want a cut of the bounty on this bitch? That's all you had to say. Have a good night—"

"Wait-wait a minute. You're already here now, so you might as well—"

"Yeah, that's what I thought, nigga," she said, pushing past him and going in the house.

I fought the urge to laugh at how predictable and slow this nigga was, but it was difficult. People who thought they were the smartest people in the room always missed what was right in front of them. The legendary bag man was no different. He quickly shut the door and led us down the hall to his home office where he closed and locked the door behind us.

"This room is soundproof, and no type of listening device works in here," he said.

"You're telling me that like either one of us is wearing a wire or looking for back-up," Mo replied, sneering at him.

"I didn't mean it like that, I just meant we can speak freely."

"Then let me say I'm gonna bury both of you bitches," I growled.

King opened his mouth to speak, but before he got a word out, Mo backhanded the spit out of my mouth. My head rocked viciously, and I tasted blood instantly, but I still smiled.

"You ain't killing shit, bitch, your days of running shit are done," Mo said.

"I thought you two were close," he said.

I could hear the suspicion in his voice, and I was betting Mo did too.

"This bitch don't respect loyalty, so she gets no more of mine. Now, how much is she worth?" Mo asked.

"The last I heard was eight figures, but it could be higher now. Hold on while I check," he replied, crossing the room to his desk.

"Move in front of me," I whispered once he was on the phone.

Mo casually moved so his vision of me was momentarily blocked, and that allowed me to get to the straight razor. I used my hands and teeth to cut my restraints off, and then I waited for the opportunity to strike. His conversation lasted about three minutes before he hung up.

"Okay, so she's worth eight figures dead or alive. How do you wanna deliver her?" he asked, coming back across the room.

I waited patiently, and when he was right next to Mo, I pushed her out of the way so I could get to him.

"You die either way this goes, so the question is, do you want your family to die too?" I asked, pushing the razor against his throat.

Aryanna

Chapter 17

King Devine was a muscular man, and he was taller than me, which might've made him think he could take me. The look in my eyes conveyed that I'd slit his throat before he could telegraph any movement to his limbs though, and I knew he could see that.

"What's it gonna be, Bag Man? Who dies?" I asked patiently.

"D-don't hurt my family."

"Okay then, all you have to do is provide the information I require. So, tell me, who is in town looking for me and my family? And where are they staying?" I asked.

"Columbians. Y-you fucked up, and they want you bad. I don't know where they are."

"But you can find them, King," Mo said.

The truth flooded his eyes, despite now badly he wanted to use his mouth to deny it.

"It's simple, King, it's their lives or those of the ones you love," I said.

When it was put to him like that, the decision wasn't hard.

"You're gonna have to let me use the phone, if you want my help," he said.

I pulled my gun out, tucked the razor in my pocket, and motioned for him to move back to his desk.

"Put it on speaker phone," I demanded, taking a seat across from him.

Mo moved to stand directly behind him, where she could watch him and the door. He placed three calls, before he got the names of the hotels around Miami and Fort Lauderdale, where the three teams of hittas were holding up.

"Three teams, huh? They must really want you dead," Mo said, impressed.

"It would seem that way. Well, King, you've been most helpful, but there's one thing I still need," I said.

"What now?"

"Open the safe," I demanded.

Aryanna

"I'd heard stories about you, Snow, but I always thought you were above the petty thuggery," he said, shaking his head as he got up and went to the safe hidden in the wall.

I chuckled softly, while he moved a picture aside and went through the required retina scan. Once the safe was open, he took a step back, and I stepped up to it. I ignored the gold-plated Smith and Wesson .45, and the stacks of hundred-dollar bills. I spotted what I was after immediately though, and I grabbed it.

"What's that?" Mo asked.

"This is his little black book," I replied smiling mischievously.

"You want his phone book?" she asked, confused.

"I said his little black book, not some phone book. This flash drive has dirt on everybody who's anybody, and this is what keeps the bag man above the law," I replied.

"Do I even wanna know how you know about that?" she asked.

I shook my head and turned to him expectantly.

"Are you really gonna make me ask you twice?" I asked.

The hatred was etched into every line in his bloodshot eyes, but I knew his self-preservation instincts would outweigh all of that. After a few deep breaths, he extended his hand for the flash drive and went back to his desk. I followed him of course and waited patiently over his shoulder, while he entered the password to decrypt the documents.

"You can move aside now," I said, once that part was done.

I sat down and quickly forwarded everything to my private email. When that was done, I wiped the computer down with a rag he had laying on the desk and stood up.

"You can shut it down now, and I'll take that flash drive just in case," I said.

I could hear him mumbling under his breath, but I didn't mind that, because I knew he wasn't paying attention to me. I quietly tucked the gun back into my pants and slid the razor back out. I waited until he'd logged off the computer before stepping up behind him, pulling his head back by his dreads, and slitting his throat in one fluid motion.

"Damn, his blood shot far!" Mo said, in awe.

I stepped to the side so I could admire the beautiful spray his life's power was making all over his desk. Some of it had shot to the middle of the floor, staining the expensive Persian rug, and that made me smile. I'd wanted to kill this motherfucker for years, but part of me had known my name had to be somewhere in his book.

"Wipe the security footage and erase any trace of us being here. I'll handle the rest," I said, heading towards the office door.

I wasn't familiar with the layout, so I crept slowly through the house, until I found Kimberly sleeping soundly in their king-size bed upstairs. King's wife was beautiful, and even in her sleep, you could tell she was full of life. I was here to fix that. Because I didn't know where the kids were in the house, or if anyone else was there, I knew the straight razor was still my safest weapon.

At the same time, I remembered Kimberly was ex-military so if I hopped on her ass, she was gonna fight to the death. I put the razor in my pocket, pulled my gun out, and tapped her on the forehead with it.

"If you scream or do anything other than what I tell you, then I'll kill you and your kids. Nod if you understand," I whispered.

She followed my directions, but I could see the anger mixed with fear in her brown eyes. I motioned her out of bed and pointed towards the door so she would know to walk in front of me out of the room.

"Go to your husband's office," I directed.

We made our way downstairs, but right before we entered the office, I smacked her in the back of the head with my pistol and pushed her inside the room. This prevented her natural reaction to scream when she saw her husband's warm body, because it was guaranteed that she was seeing stars right now. I quickly shut the door behind us, and then I moved to stand over Kimberly.

"Since you know your husband was the bag man, I'm sure you're not surprised to end up in this situation," I said.

"We don't have anything to do with this business," she replied.

"And yet, here you are. I want you to know it's not personal though, it's just business," I said.

Aryanna

She opened her mouth to speak, and I shot her in it. I put two more bullets in her head after her body dropped, just to make sure she was gone.

"You finished?" Mo asked.

"I was waiting on you," I replied, tucking my gun back in my pants.

We made our way out of the house as quickly and quietly as we'd come and moments later, we were in my car driving smoothly away.

"Where to now?" Mo asked.

"We've got one more stop to make in order to kick this party off."

"Oh yeah, and where is that, oh wise mysterious one?" she asked, laughing.

"Laugh now, bitch, because so much blood is about to fly, won't shit be funny for years to come."

My statement had a sobering affect, and we rode on in silence for a while. I understood that for the Columbians to send three different hit teams, it meant they wanted to make one hundred percent sure me and my family stopped breathing. I wasn't exactly sure how I went up against a force that strong or determined, but I knew the only way to eat an elephant was one bite at a time.

"So, where are we going?" she asked seriously.

"We're going to see Mike."

"Mike...you mean Whitty, the nigga who swears he's some type of boss in these streets?" she asked, looking at me like I was crazy.

"Yeah, that Mike."

"Um, not to question your logic or anything, Snow, but why exactly are we going to see him?"

"Because he's the perfect salesman, and we need to sell the idea I've left Florida for good," I replied.

"And you think he's gonna do you this favor for free, or because he's a nice guy?"

"Of course not. That nigga is a pussy hound and wannabe ladies' man, so I'm about to gas his frail ego and then fuck him real quick," I said smiling.

This time when she started laughing, I didn't say or do anything to stop her, I just kept driving. We arrived at our destination half an hour later.

"It's four a.m., Snow, what makes you think that this nigga ain't laid up with some bitch right now?"

I laughed aloud before answering.

"Even if he was, and that's a big-ass if, you know the bitch ain't badder than me," I replied arrogantly.

"True. So, how we playing this?"

"You're gonna ring the doorbell," I said.

This had both of us laughing as we got out of the car. We crept up on his house like car burglars, pulling our pistols out along the way. Once we made it up on the porch, I gave her the nod to ring the bell. She complied and a few seconds later, some lights came on.

"Who the fuck is it?"

"Put your glasses on, you blind bastard," Mo replied, shaking her head.

A few moments later, the door opened and the biggest bug I'd ever seen poked his head out.

"Damn, them glasses are thick as fuck!" I said, laughing as I raised my gun.

"Can you see these guns, Mike?" Mo asked, waving hers in front of him.

"Do I know you?" he asked.

"Very funny," Mo said, pushing past him.

I followed her lead into the house and took a seat beside her on the couch.

"What can you do for me, Snow?" he asked, crossing his arms over his stocky frame.

"What can I do for you?"

Aryanna

"Yeah. I mean, you gotta be waking me up in the middle of the night, because you can do something for me. Unless you just wanna spend some time with me," he replied smiling.

"What's going on, Mikey?"

This question came from the white girl who had just stumbled out of the back room, rubbing sleep from her eyes.

"Baby, go back to bed, I—"

Before he could finish his sentence, I'd raised my pistol and put a neat hole through her left eyebrow. Her body dropped fast, but his reaction was slow. He looked at her, then looked at me and back to her again.

"That wasn't necessary, Snow. You can't just come in my house and shoot my guests, slim."

"Well, look at it like this. If she was in your bed, then there would be no room for us," I said.

"Us!" they replied in unison.

I chuckled softly, while giving Mo a look to encourage her to play along.

"I mean, if you think her pussy was better than either one of ours, then we'll just leave. Her body is still warm," I said.

"You know I ain't say all that, Snow, I was just-I mean, I was surprised to see you two here, that's all. You ain't gotta leave though, just tell me how you wanna do this."

"The same way we do everything else, nigga, business before pleasure," Mo said.

"Okay, what's the business that brings you two my way?"

"I need you to spread the word that me and my team have left Florida for good," I replied.

"And who am I telling this to?"

"Anybody who will listen," Mo replied.

"Cool. Let me grab my phone and get on that."

"Do it out here with us, so you can keep us company," I said, sensually.

The stupid smile that popped up on his face told me that he actually believed the bullshit I'd just spoon-fed him. As soon as he left the room, Mo turned to me.

"Us! You got this nigga thinking he's about to fuck the both of us, bitch?" she asked, in a furious whisper.

"Calm down, bitch. The only pussy that nigga is getting is from that dead bitch over there," I replied in the same tone.

I could see the skepticism in her eyes, but I knew she knew better than to think we were here to literally fuck this nigga. Wack niggas didn't get pussy unless they paid for it, and no amount of money was gonna make me give it up to Mikey boy.

He came back into the room with his phone already up to his ear and took a seat on the love seat across from us. I knew this wasn't a matter of making a simple phone call, so I pulled out my own phone and settled in for a while.

I checked in with my people to make sure everything was quiet, and our arrival had gone undetected. I provided the locations of the teams of hittas to Red Gunz, Vontrell, and J5 with the instructions to have some inconspicuous people scout them. When that conversation was over, I checked the stash houses to see how much work was left, and to see if the coke had arrived as Phillisa had promised. I was pleasantly surprised to find things running like clockwork.

My calls only took me about thirty minutes, but Mike was still on his phone doing his thing. I could tell by the way Mo was watching him that she was listening to every word coming out of his mouth. I liked that about her, but boredom put a bad idea in my head that I impulsively acted upon.

Without a word, I scooted closer to her and then wrapped my arms around her. She didn't resist, but I could tell that she was still concentrating. When I started kissing her neck softly her breathing changed, and Mike's eyes somehow got bigger behind the projection screens he called glasses.

"Snow, s-stop playing," she mumbled.

"Just do what you're doing, bitch, and that goes for you too, Mike."

"I'm good over here, slim. You just keep doing what you're doing," he replied, smiling widely.

I continued kissing her neck with my eyes locked on Mike's. He fucked up in the conversation he was having twice, and that made me chuckle. I paused in what I was doing, and just stared at Mike.

"What?" he asked.

"I need you to focus on what you're supposed to be doing, and you can join us as soon as you're done," I replied.

He didn't bother responding, he just went back to his conversation.

"Come here," I said to Mo, pulling her towards me and sitting my gun down next to me.

When she turned to face me, I kissed her passionately, while sliding my left hand quickly inside her pants.

"You're such a bitch for this," she said, sighing as I began to rub her clit.

I worked her delicate hidden jewel in a slow clockwise motion, while alternating between sucking on her bottom lip and nibbling it. I could hear Mike talking with the speed and persuasiveness of an experienced salesman / dopeboy, and I smiled briefly.

"Pass me your gun," I whispered.

She put it in my right hand, and I sat it next to mine in plain sight for Mike to see. I caught the gasp that escaped Mo's mouth when I pushed two fingers inside her tight pussy. I worked quickly, like someone who knew the body they were playing like a symphony, enjoying how rapidly the storm inside her was building.

"Cl-Claudette," she moaned, gripping my arm tightly with both of her hands.

"Shhhhhh, bae, just cum for me."

My demand made her grind against my hand, and that made me work my finger faster.

"Ohh-oh shit," she cried out, throwing her head towards the ceiling.

"Ay, uh, I'm done, Snow. I did what you needed," he said.

"You sure?" I asked, never pausing in what I was doing to Mo.

"Yeah, I put the word out with everyone I could think of to tell."

"Good job, Mikey...do you wanna make her cum for me?" I asked.

"Hell yeah!"

"S-Snow, wait," Mo pleaded.

"It's okay, bae," I assured her, unbuttoning her shirt.

Mike came over to us and stood there with the evidence of his arousal only a few inches away from my face.

"Suck her titties, Mike, that does it for her," I said.

"Snow!" Mo said, grabbing me tighter.

"It's okay," I said, casually shaking my arm loose from her grip.

Mike wasted no time pulling her bra down until her titties spilled free. He was so mesmerized by her perfect breasts and light brown nipples that he never saw me pick up my gun. I put it to the side of his head and pulled the trigger. His brains and blood shot all over Mo, but she had her eyes closed because she was cumming.

"F-fuck bitch, my mouth could've been open," she said, breathlessly.

All I did was laugh, and push Mike's body away from us so that I could get a better angle.

"I'll make up for it by giving you one more nut before we leave," I said.

"H-hurry the fuck up."

Aryanna

Chapter 18

Two days later

"You look just like your sister," I said, staring across the table at JoJo Davenport.

"I think like her too, so maybe you can help me understand why my sister would go into business with you, Snow. We both know she wasn't your biggest fan."

"True, but she respected the fact that I spared her life when Campa wanted me to kill her, and everything that looked like her, for that matter. She didn't owe me anything though, and we'd worked out a new business arrangement."

"Which was?" she asked.

"I agreed to supply her."

My response solicited no immediate response, but I could see the wheels turning behind her golden-green eyes. I'd done my homework on Nicki's twin sister, and I'd discovered that she was with the shit as much as Nicki had been. So, the only question was if she was trying to be a part of the team.

"For me to get involved, I'd need to know that you're gonna honor the deal you made with my sister," she said.

"With you, Chief Petty Officer Second Class Davenport?"

"Ah, so you did a Google search on me?" she asked smiling.

"I dug a little deeper than that, JoJo. I know you used to pimp girls, give massages with happy endings, dance at the Pink Pony, escort professional athletes around the world, and slang a little dope. You're a jack of all trades."

"I mastered some of them too, but I'm sure you found that out while you were digging," she said, non-plussed by my revelations.

"I found out something more important than all of that though. I found out that you can keep your mouth shut, and I value that."

She nodded her head in agreement and understanding.

"So with all that being said, yeah, I can keep my agreement I made with Nicki. Are you sure you can handle the quantity she was looking for?"

"I won't lie, it's probably more than I've dealt with before, but I've found it to be true that good dope sells itself. Texas is wide open for the taking, because the cartels care more about killing each other, than turning a hard profit. I care about that bottom line," she replied.

"I respect that. First things first, we've gotta win the war we're in."

"Tell me how I can help," she said amicably.

"Your sister provided essential information. Do you think you can do the same?"

"Who do you think Nicki called first when she needed something? I got you, all you gotta do is say what you need. Just make sure you don't try to fuck me, Snow."

"Oh, really? So, we can't mix business with pleasure?" I asked smiling.

"You know what I'm saying to you. We can eat each other's pussies until one of us taps out, but what we ain't gonna do is fuck each other over. Feel me?"

"I feel you, JoJo."

She stuck her hand across the table, and I shook it. With that settled, I summoned the waiter back to us so our orders could be taken. It had been JoJo's idea to meet out in the open, but with everything that was going on, I'd suggested a compromise of a sit-down at a restaurant I had closed to the public. Mo had tried to insist that she be present, but I needed her at the house. Our compromise had been that Fatz could tag along, and he was currently holding up the wall across the room, staring at the back of JoJo's head. Once we ordered, I called him over to me with a wave of the hand.

"We're good. I want you to call Mo and tell her to get a care package together for JoJo. Also, tell her to have a room set up for JoJo to stay in while she's in town."

"I'm good at my hotel, Snow—"

"No, you're not. The people who are coming for us have a long reach," Fatz said.

"Will you protect me?" she asked seductively.

"Don't do that," I said.

"Do what, Snow?"

"Don't flirt with him, he's taken," I said calmly.

"If he's taken, then he can speak for himself," she replied smiling.

"Joanna, do I look like I'm playing with you? Because I'm not, and I hate to repeat myself."

"It's okay, Snow, I'll handle it," Fatz said, taking a seat next to JoJo.

"I want you to listen to me carefully, JoJo. I'm sooooo not interested, and that's not a shot at you. You're a beautiful woman, and I'm sure you know how to put it down in the bedroom. But the facts are that I'm in a committed relationship, and I love my woman."

"I understand, and I respect your honesty. She is a lucky woman," JoJo said.

"Now that we got that out of the way, let me tell you what I need first," I said.

We discussed the most pressing business of how to eliminate the immediate threats and keep tabs on all other players in this equation. When that was done, we got down to the business of where to send the "care package" full of coke that I was giving her, on the strength of our new business agreement. Fatz excused himself to take care of that, and by the time he came back we were ready to leave.

"You can follow us to the house, and I'll send somebody to get your stuff from your hotel room later," I said.

"Okay. I need to bring a friend of mine out here to assist me though."

"Who is this friend?" I asked.

"Wild Strawberry. She's a dancer that's also a hitta, and I trust her with my life," JoJo replied.

"You might be betting your life on her, because if she's not who she says she is, I'll bury the both of you."

I could tell my words didn't offend her by the look of understanding in her eyes, and that made me like her more. We left the restaurant with me and Fatz in my Lamborghini, and JoJo following us in her red Mustang.

Aryanna

"So, what do you think?" I asked.

"I think you're going about this the right way, and you're prepared for what comes next. No matter what, you know we're riding with you."

"I know this nigga," I said, pushing him playfully.

He pushed me back at the exact same time that something smacked my windshield hard. I was about to ask him if he'd seen what the hell it was, when the repeated tap of bullets made themselves known. I quickly flicked the pedals attached to my steering wheel to shift gears and mashed the gas pedal to the floor.

"Where are the shots coming from?" he asked.

"I don't know, but I think it's a sniper in a building."

When he pulled his pistol, I thought he was about to let the window down to shoot, but he kept it in his lap while his eyes scanned everything. I looked in the rearview mirror and saw JoJo was struggling to keep up with the speed and power of my million-dollar toy. But, slowing down wasn't an option.

"Text JoJo and tell her to break away from us, and keep driving until I call her," I said, tossing him my phone.

My eyes never left the road, and that's how I was able to spot the two SUV's, trying to box me in at the intersection we were approaching. I shifted gears, faster than any race car driver, and picked up enough speed to thread the needle to shoot between them. The sigh of relief never got past my tongue though, because there were two cop cars on the opposite side of the road, headed in my direction. I tried to hit the brakes to reduce my speed, but a glance at the speedometer showed I was doing one hundred twenty-five miles per hour. If I thought it was a malfunction, the flashing lights in front of me shattered that allusion.

"Put your gun away," I said, slowing down to wait for the cops who just pulled a one-eighty in the middle of the street. The sound of sirens floated through the air to announce their pursuit, but I was already pulling over to the curb.

"Keep your eyes open in case those crazy motherfuckers try something with the cops right here," I said.

A Dope Boy's Queen 2

I grabbed my title out of the glove compartment, and my license out of my wallet. Then I waited. I wasn't worried about the gun I had at the small of my back, because I was licensed to carry a firearm. The only problem was that this particular gun wasn't registered to me. I was just glad it wasn't the same one I'd used on Mike the other day.

"What the fuck is taking so long?" Fatz asked, after we'd been sitting for a few minutes.

When two more cop cars pulled up in front of us a few seconds later, we had our answer. They got out immediately, with their guns aimed at my car.

"Don't move," I whispered.

"The car's bulletproof, but I had no intentions on moving anyway."

"Driver! Open your door and step out slowly!"

This command came from the car behind me, and when I looked in the rearview mirror again, I found two more guns pointed at us.

"Why do I get the feeling this ain't about a speeding ticket?" I asked.

"Because it's not. The question is, are these real cops?"

That thought hadn't crossed my mind until this exact moment, and it made me analyze the whole situation differently.

"Driver! Get out of the car now!"

"Snow..."

I could hear the worry in Fatz's voice, and I knew it wasn't because he was afraid of the real police. I had a decision to make in this moment, and I knew what the right decision was. I swiftly put the car back into gear and stepped on the gas pedal. Shots rained down immediately, but they bounced off just as fast. I swerved to avoid hitting either cop car in front of me, hitting the first corner I came to.

"Where are we going?" he asked.

"To the police station."

"You're fucking with me, right?" he asked, looking at me.

"No, I'm not. If those were real cops, then they'll follow us there and if they're not, then we'll get them off our ass for the moment. Use my phone, and start shooting the chase on Instagram."

"Smart thinking," he replied.

Once he had the phone ready and Instagram up, he turned towards me.

"This is Attorney Claudette Snow. I'm currently being chased by Miami-Dade police, or some people posing as police. I've been shot at without provocation, and for that reason, I'm now fleeing from them. If I die, just know I didn't do a damn thing to deserve it."

I nodded at Fatz and he turned my phone so everyone could see the cop cars in pursuit through my back window. I could've easily outrun them, but that would've defeated the purpose. Ten minutes later, when I slid to a stop out front of the police station, the cop cars were still behind me, and there were more cops positioned out front with their guns out.

"Well, I guess they're real cops," I said, looking around and shaking my head.

"Yeah, but that still doesn't explain why they're on your ass, or why they shot at you."

His points were valid, but the guessing game was over. I put my gun under the driver's seat and opened my door, but I didn't step out until he had my phone pointed back at me.

"My hands are up and I'm unarmed!" I yelled, before I stepped out into the afternoon sunshine.

"Walk forward with your hands high," a cop demanded from a few feet away.

I did as I was told and a few moments later, I was surrounded by men with guns.

"Get on your knees."

"Oh no, you got me fucked up," I said, shaking my head.

A cop stepped forward and quickly put me in handcuffs before leading me up the steps. When we walked into the building, all eyes were on us and everyone stopped what they were doing. I was well known, and the looks of uncertainty I saw in a lot of eyes, told me they couldn't believe they were seeing me in this situation.

"Put her in an interrogation room," a man in a suit said, coming from behind the front desk.

I was led into the back, and it felt weird as shit, but I was familiar with the routine all the same. I was shoved roughly into a chair and left alone, with just the one-way mirror to keep me company. I knew all the tactics and games the cops would play, so sweating was something I wouldn't do. My time was better spent trying to figure out what the fuck was going on.

Part of me had thought JoJo had set me up, but that was eighty-five percent paranoia, and fifteen percent logical deduction. That didn't make any percent of it real though. My money was definitely on Campa, but at the same time, I would never underestimate Phillisa ever again. Whoever or whatever, it was didn't matter because, I was too good of a lawyer to get put in a trick bag.

I leaned my head back against the wall and closed my eyes to settle in for the wait. I couldn't be sure how much time passed, but I'd damn near fallen asleep by the time I heard the door open again. The man in the suit, who'd picked the location I was in, came into the room and sat across from me.

"My name is Agent Reddish, and I work for the FBI."

I looked across the desk at the neatly put together, middle aged, slender built man, trying to evaluate how this was about to play out.

"Do you know why we had you detained, Mrs. Snow?"

"I haven't the foggiest idea, Agent Reddish, but I'd sure like to know."

"Well, it would seem you're not who you appear to be Claudette."

"I'm just a businesswoman and entrepreneur," I replied smiling.

"Now, if that were true, then you wouldn't have a stack of dead bodies scattered around you. You also wouldn't have people constantly trying to kill you, now would you?"

"I just happened to be in the wrong place, at the wrong time, Agent Reddish."

Aryanna

"You know, that's exactly what I thought before I started looking into you. You're an excellent trial lawyer, and your record speaks for itself. So, it would stand to reason you would come into contact with some unsavory characters, but that doesn't make you a bad person or an accomplice to anything. The part that puzzled me was how you would be able to take the mansion of a known kingpin without being with the shit. Then the answer came to me immediately…you are with the shit. Aren't you, Claudette?"

I just smiled at him because we both knew I'd never answer any incriminating questions.

"Yeah, I figured that would be your response, which is why I kept doing my homework. That's how I discovered the relationship between Zion Snow, and Campa," he said.

I kept my smile in place, but I could feel my eye twitching slightly.

"Zion was your husband, right?"

"You know the answer to that question, so make your point."

"My point is that you're up to your pretty little neck in all the bullshit that's going on in Miami. My point is that you need help, and I can help you," he said.

"Agent Reddish, you sound so sincere about that. I almost wanna…no-no, I don't wanna help you, because I don't know what the fuck you're talking about."

This time it was him that smiled at me, and it made me feel uneasy.

"Have you ever heard the saying that every group has a Judas?" he asked.

I'd definitely heard that before, but I knew the tactics that the government used.

"What's your point, Agent?"

"No point, Mrs. Snow. Do you wanna cooperate?"

"There's nothing for me to cooperate with."

"You're right. Please stand up for me and face the wall," he requested politely.

I did what he wanted, but when he took my handcuffs off, I was confused. I turned around and looked at him, preparing to take my ass whooping head-up.

"You're free to go," he said.

"Huh?"

"I said, you're free to go, but I want you to remember something. I tried to save your life. When you go missing, I won't try again."

Aryanna

A Dope Boy's Queen 2

Chapter 19

When Agent Reddish walked out of the room and left me standing there, I thought it was some type of trick. As the minutes ticked by though, and no one came to put cuffs back on me, I started to feel free again. I walked from the room, and back out into the reception area. No one paused in their tasks or even spared a glance in my direction, but I was more than okay with that. When I walked out front, I spotted Fatz pacing back and forth, on the phone. I could tell by how animated he was that whoever he was talking to was pissing him off, but as soon as he saw me, he hung up.

"Are you okay?" he asked, moving towards me and scooping me up in a bear hug.

"I'm good. Some really weird shit just happened, but I'm good, so let's get the fuck out of here."

"I'll drive," he said, carrying me to the car before putting me on my feet.

I got in, he got behind the wheel and a few seconds later, we were leaving a cloud of smoke in the police parking lot.

"What the fuck is going on, Snow?"

"I honestly don't know. When they dragged me inside, there was an FBI agent waiting on me."

"FBI? What the hell could the feds want with you?" he asked, looking over at me.

"He said he wanted to help me, but you know like I do, that's a bunch of bullshit. I would say they're shooting in the dark, but this motherfucker knew too much already. He said something to me about me taking Campa's house, Zion working for Campa, and me being mixed up in the illegal shit going on in Miami."

"Oh shit, Snow."

"Yeah, that about sums up how I'm feeling right now. Then, when I refused his help, he says some fucked-up shit. He says that every group has a Judas."

"You mean, as in—"

"Yeah, he's saying someone on my team is snitching," I said.

Aryanna

Saying it out loud left both of us without words. Things were entirely too crazy right now for me to have to worry about a god-damn rat in my circle! I'd always known the probability of this problem arising, it was just fucked-up timing right now.

"So, how do you wanna handle this?" he asked.

"Do you still have my phone?"

He dug in his pocket and passed it to me. My first call was to Vegas to check on things out there and make the necessary changes to the plans I'd put in motion. When that was done, I called Mo and told her I wanted a meeting with everybody within the next hour. She agreed to make it happen, and then asked for my version of what happened earlier. I ran it down to her, answered her questions and hung up.

"I don't know why she's asking you the same shit I just told her," Fatz said.

I could hear the irritation in his voice, but I wasn't gonna feed into it.

"She's just being thorough, Fatz. Right now, we need the people we can trust to be on top of the game, like Jordan in his prime."

He didn't respond, but the look he had on his face softened. I texted my address to JoJo so she could meet us and twenty minutes later, we were pulling up to my house.

"What the fuck was that?" JoJo asked, hopping out of her car as soon as she saw us.

"I wish I knew. The first part was obviously Campa's people trying to avenge him, because by now they're assuming he's dead. The second part was some shit that I gotta look into," I replied.

"I had no idea what the hell was going on until the shit was all over the 'Gram. I thought for sure your ass was done!" she said, shaking her head.

"It won't be that easy. Come on," I said, leading the way into the house.

One of the best things about this property Mo had purchased for me was that it was in a gated community, and my house sat all the way in the back, away from the others. It was impossible to sneak up on my spot. When we walked in, I could hear the sounds of

A Dope Boy's Queen 2

multiple voices, and that was the direction I headed in. The first person I spotted was Meatrock, and his eyes got as big as softballs when he saw JoJo. It was Mo, Phillisa, Gunz, J5, Vontrell, Aubrey, Aaron, and a nigga I didn't recognize sitting around the living room.

"Who is this?" I asked, nodding at the brown-skinned nigga smoking a big blunt.

"I'm Duke, Silk's brother."

I evaluated him with the same steady gaze he was using on me. His build wasn't imposing when you first looked at him, but the broad chest and obvious height would prove useful if he was a warrior.

"What are you, about six foot one, maybe two-hundred-twenty pounds?" I asked.

"You got a good eye," he replied.

"Duke was just telling us he did a little boxing when he was in Philly," Aubrey said.

I knew without looking at Aubrey or Aaron, that they wanted a piece of young Duke. Not because he'd done anything, but because he was speaking their language.

"Were you any good, Duke?" I asked.

"Still am good," he replied, smiling through the cloud of smoke escaping his mouth.

Since I had no interest in discussing new business in front of two virtual strangers, I formulated a quick plan in my mind.

"I've got some business to handle, but Duke, you're more than welcome to hang out with Aaron and Aubrey for a little while."

"No disrespect, but I didn't come here to hang out. I came to get the nigga who killed my brother," he said.

"We all understand that, but to honest with you, I'm having trust issues right now. I don't know you, so I'm not about to discuss my business in front of you," I said.

He chuckled softly while standing up.

"I respect your honesty. Are you sure you wanna put your dogs in the ring with a wolf though?" he asked, looking at Aubrey and Aaron.

I looked at them and found wide grins on both of their faces.

Aryanna

"Yeah, I'm good with that," I replied.

"Alright then," Duke said, passing me the blunt as he walked past me, following Aubrey and Aaron out of the room.

"Meatrock, why don't you show JoJo the house," Mo suggested.

"Oh-okay," he said, trying to hide his excitement.

Once they left, I addressed everyone left.

"I've got the location of the hittas that came to kill us, so were gonna hit all three locations at the same time. Phillisa, I need you to put together a team in Columbia, because the only way to end this is to go at the head of the snake. I'm not trying to be looking over my shoulder forever," I said.

"I've gotta run that past the committee first, Snow," Phillisa said.

"And yet, you're still here," Mo said.

The look they exchanged was beyond ugly, but it got Phillisa to pull out her phone and walk off a little.

"We're gonna split up as follows: Fatz, Mo, me, and Gunz's team will run down on one hotel. J5, I want your team, Aubrey, and Aaron to hit another hotel. Vontrell, that leaves your team, Meatrock, and Phillisa on the last spot. Depending on how Duke shakes out with the ass whooping he's about to get, he might join one of your teams. Any questions?"

All eyes were on me, but no one said anything.

"We strike at dawn," I said.

"So, are we just running up in the hotel and laying shit down, or are we blowing up the whole building?" Gunz asked.

"If we take out the whole building, then we'll be labelled terrorists, and that ain't something I'm trying to get hit with," I replied honestly.

"I agree, we need to hit who we came for and vanish," Fatz said.

"There will be witnesses," Gunz warned.

"That's unavoidable, unfortunately. So, I'll plan our escape route, because once we hit them, we're gonna take a long vacation," I replied.

A Dope Boy's Queen 2

"You sure Vegas is far enough now that you've got the feds sniffing around?" Mo asked.

"Feds?" Gunz asked, looking at me for an explanation.

I quickly ran down what had happened on the way here, and when I was done, a hush fell over everyone.

"It may not be my place to ask this question, but with all of that going on, do you really think it's a good idea to drop these bodies here and now?" J5 asked.

"Do you think the contract killers that were sent here by the cartel to torture and kill me, are gonna wait around for the feds to leave town?" I retorted.

"Touché," J5 said.

"Okay, so let's discuss the locations and see about getting the layouts so we can plan how to attack," I suggested, leading the way from the living room to the dining room.

We all took seats around the large oak table, and I had Mo pull the hotels up on her tablet. We were fifteen minutes into our strategy session when Aaron, Aubrey, and Duke strolled back into the room laughing and joking. All three of them had a busted lip, and at least one bleeding cut in their faces, but no one was mad.

"How did he do?" I asked.

"I hold my own, no matter who my opponent is," Duke said arrogantly.

"I don't know who trained him, but he can fight," Aubrey conceded.

The look in Aubrey's eyes told me he meant what he'd said, but I knew better than to doubt his sincerity anyway.

"Grab a seat, we were just putting a plan together," I said.

"Snow, can I holla at you real quick?" Phillisa called from the doorway.

My eyes locked on Mo, and I could tell she was about to get up, but I shook my head to keep her seated. I got up and stepped into the hallway where Phillisa stood, holding her phone in her hand.

"What is it?"

"They-uh, they want you to come to Columbia for a sit-down," she replied.

"Did you explain that now is not the time for that?"

"I did, but...you know I answer to them," she said, holding her hands up.

"Then what fucking good are you to me? I'm a boss bitch, and if you ain't on my level, then you're in the goddamn way," I said angrily, turning around and going back into the dining room.

We spent an hour devising plans of attack, before breaking up to start putting shit together. When the meeting of the minds was done, everyone except for me and Fatz left to handle the business. I wanted to be on the front line, but with the Feds watching I had to lay low until the curtain went up. Fatz stayed to make sure I wasn't alone if some unexpected attack came, while Mo was in the field running shit.

"This waiting around shit is for the birds," I said, forcing myself to sit down on the couch and stop pacing.

"Try being locked up."

"I keep forgetting you did a bid, so I'm sorry for sounding like a poor little rich girl."

"That's not how you sound, Snow, you sound like a war general who wants to be out there putting that work in with her soldiers."

"I do," I admitted.

"I've been there before. The hardest part of my time was the last year inside, because I had to swallow a lot of shit, and act like it was sugar. I couldn't react the way I was accustomed to because that meant setting my time back, or not coming home at all. So, I was forced to learn some discipline and patience, neither of which is easy to come by."

"Tell me about it," I said, shaking my head.

"The trick is to do something to occupy your time and take your mind off the nothingness."

I thought about that for a minute, and then considered what I wanted to do. After a few moments, the best idea came to me.

"Come on," I said, getting up off the couch and making my way to the kitchen.

I went straight to the refrigerator, and thanked Mo silently for making sure it was fully stocked.

"Uh, what are you about to do?" he asked, hesitantly.

"Cook for us, and you're helping."

His laughter was genuine, but he didn't run away.

"So, what are we cooking?" he asked from behind me.

"Uh, from the looks of it, there are some pork chops in here, so look for a vegetable in the cabinet."

I pulled the pack of pork chops out and sat them on the counter, while I gathered everything else that I'd need to fry them.

"Is corn okay, Snow?"

"Yeah and see if there are some instant potatoes in there too."

He brought out everything and put it on the counter. Then, he surprised the shit out of me by actually washing his hands and starting to prep the meal.

"You're seriously gonna help me?" I asked, washing my hands too.

"That's what you said, right? Do you think I don't know how to cook?"

"No, I-I just thought…never mind," I said, laughing softly.

It only took us half an hour to whip up the simple meal, and then we took it to the dining room table.

"If we had some wine, we'd be in business," he said.

His statement froze me in the middle of sitting down as the last night I'd spent with Zion came rushing towards me out of the darkness.

"Snow, are you okay?"

"I-I-I'm…"

I wanted to say I was fine, but the tightness in my chest prevented me from saying anything. The sudden feeling of Fatz's hands on me snapped me out of my trance, and I could feel my heart hammering inside my chest. I looked up to find his brown eyes full of concern.

"I'm f-fine. I just had a random memory pop up," I said.

"That must've been some hell of a memory."

"It was. The last time I had sex with my husband was on the night he was killed, and we did it on our dining room table," I confessed.

Fatz smiled down at me, but the memory didn't make me smile.

"I thought I had the perfect life then, but he had another bitch, and another child," I said softly, looking down to hide the tears I could feel in my eyes.

Fatz didn't say anything at first, but then he took my chin in his hand, and forced me to look at him.

"He was stupid, Snow, and if he was that stupid then, he never deserved you in the first place."

I was on the verge of defending Zion out of habit, but before I could, Fatz was kissing me. The shock I felt froze my body, but my mouth was working on its own, because my pussy was dripping instantly. Part of me wanted to resist what my body so obviously needed, because I hadn't discussed this with Mo, but I didn't know how to stop.

There wasn't a conscious thought in my mind to put my hand into his pants, and yet I could feel the hardness of his dick across my palm. The change in his breathing when I slowly started moving my hand up and down made my heart beat faster. When he unbuttoned my pants, I thought he had the same intentions as me but instead, he pushed my pants and panties down over my hips. The air caressing my naked flesh gave me goosebumps and sent a shill up my spine. Suddenly, the whole temperature of the mood changed. He spun me around, and I had to use my hands to stop myself from going face first onto the table.

"Open your legs," he demanded, grabbing me by my neck roughly.

My compliance happened without conscious thought, and the next thing I knew, his dick was plowing into me. The grip he had on my throat wasn't tight, but I was still having trouble breathing under the steady strokes he was feeding me. There were no words to describe the thrill of his power over me in this moment, and it was something I gave into without reservation.

"That's right, take this dick," he growled, fucking me harder.

I could feel my body coming alive with the speed that night gives way to sunrise. The trembling in my arms told me I might be on my face soon, but I didn't care as long as he kept up the beautiful punishment.

"Faster," I moaned, closing my eyes as I chased my orgasm.

His grip on my throat tightened, while his other hand went to my hip so he could hold me steady. From that point, all I knew was the beautiful savagery of his pound game. Within minutes, my pussy spasmed and gushed so hard, I could feel my teeth rattling.

"So, this is what you two do without me?"

Our bodies froze, but nothing could stop my rolling orgasm, and I felt Fatz's cum shoot inside me with a bullet's force. I could tell it was a struggle for him to pull out of me, but he managed it, and we both turned around to find Mo standing in the dining room doorway.

Aryanna

Chapter 20

"M-Mo, it ain't what you think," I said, pulling up my pants and straightening my clothes.

"Really? That's good, because from where I'm standing, it looks like you were fucking my nigga."

"Baby, I—"

"Shut up, Fatz," she said, focusing on me.

"We didn't plan this and honestly, I didn't think you'd mind," I said.

"I only mind because I didn't know. If you would've come to me first, then I wouldn't feel like you motherfuckers were sneaking around behind my back."

"Baby, I—"

"Shut up, Fatz," I said.

This time he wisely took a step back and let her and me have this conversation.

"I'm sorry, Anastasia, and I mean that," I said sincerely.

For a moment, she simply stood there looking at me and then she walked away. Fatz moved to follow her, but I waved him off as I followed her footsteps.

"Mo?" I called after her.

She didn't pause or turn around, she just kept heading for the front door. I finally caught up with her out front before she could get in the car.

"Anastasia!"

"What the fuck do you want, Claudette?" she asked, spinning around on me like she wanted to fight.

"I'm sorry," I said contritely.

"No you're not, bitch, you never are. You're all about yourself. What Snow wants, what Snow needs, and it's fuck everybody else. So, you fucking my nigga is just par for the course. I should've expected it though because you ain't shit, just like your dirty dick dead husband."

I could feel my mouth hanging open in shock, but that quickly morphed into anger.

Aryanna

"You know what, bitch, fuck you! You're just mad because my pussy makes your nigga weak and your pussy makes niggas flee," I said, turning around and walking away.

I didn't expect to see Fatz standing a few feet away, and the expression on his face told me he'd heard everything we'd said. His eyes were on Mo, and when his gaze turned to me, he pulled his gun out. I put my hands up to somehow ward off the bullet I knew was coming, but the sound of the roaring cannon came from behind me instead of from him. Before Fatz hit the ground, I spun back around to Mo, knowing I owed her for saving my life. I was about to open my mouth to verbalize that, when I realized she was aiming at me next.

"I should've done this a long fucking time ago, bitch. You're not fit to be queen of this empire," she said.

I closed my eyes as the sound of the gun going off echoed in my ears…

To Be Continued…
A Dope Boy's Queen 3
Coming Soon

Submission Guideline

Submit the first three chapters of your completed manuscript to ldpsubmissions@gmail.com, subject line: Your book's title. The manuscript must be in a .doc file and sent as an attachment. Document should be in Times New Roman, double spaced and in size 12 font. Also, provide your synopsis and full contact information. If sending multiple submissions, they must each be in a separate email.

Have a story but no way to send it electronically? You can still submit to LDP/Ca$h Presents. Send in the first three chapters, written or typed, of your completed manuscript to:

**LDP: Submissions Dept
Po Box 944
Stockbridge, Ga 30281**

DO NOT send original manuscript. Must be a duplicate.

Provide your synopsis and a cover letter containing your full contact information.

Thanks for considering LDP and Ca$h Presents.

Aryanna

Coming Soon from Lock Down Publications/Ca$h Presents

BOW DOWN TO MY GANGSTA
By **Ca$h**
TORN BETWEEN TWO
By **Coffee**
THE STREETS STAINED MY SOUL **II**
By **Marcellus Allen**
BLOOD OF A BOSS **VI**
SHADOWS OF THE GAME II
By **Askari**
LOYAL TO THE GAME **IV**
By **T.J. & Jelissa**
A DOPEBOY'S PRAYER **II**
By **Eddie "Wolf" Lee**
IF LOVING YOU IS WRONG… **III**
By **Jelissa**
TRUE SAVAGE **VII**
MIDNIGHT CARTEL III
DOPE BOY MAGIC IV
CITY OF KINGZ II
By **Chris Green**
BLAST FOR ME **III**
A SAVAGE DOPEBOY III
CUTTHROAT MAFIA III
By **Ghost**
A HUSTLER'S DECEIT III
KILL ZONE **II**
BAE BELONGS TO ME III
A DOPE BOY'S QUEEN III

A Dope Boy's Queen 2

By **Aryanna**
COKE KINGS V
KING OF THE TRAP II

By **T.J. Edwards**
GORILLAZ IN THE BAY V

De'Kari
THE STREETS ARE CALLING II

Duquie Wilson
KINGPIN KILLAZ IV
STREET KINGS III
PAID IN BLOOD III
CARTEL KILLAZ IV
DOPE GODS III

Hood Rich
SINS OF A HUSTLA II

ASAD
KINGZ OF THE GAME V

Playa Ray
SLAUGHTER GANG IV
RUTHLESS HEART IV

By Willie Slaughter
THE HEART OF A SAVAGE III

By Jibril Williams
FUK SHYT II

By Blakk Diamond
THE REALEST KILLAZ II

By Tranay Adams
TRAP GOD II

By Troublesome
YAYO IV

Aryanna

A SHOOTER'S AMBITION III
By S. Allen
GHOST MOB
Stilloan Robinson
KINGPIN DREAMS III
By Paper Boi Rari
CREAM
By Yolanda Moore
SON OF A DOPE FIEND III
By Renta
FOREVER GANGSTA II
GLOCKS ON SATIN SHEETS III
By Adrian Dulan
LOYALTY AIN'T PROMISED II
By Keith Williams
THE PRICE YOU PAY FOR LOVE II
DOPE GIRL MAGIC III
By Destiny Skai
CONFESSIONS OF A GANGSTA II
By Nicholas Lock
I'M NOTHING WITHOUT HIS LOVE II
By Monet Dragun
LIFE OF A SAVAGE IV
A GANGSTA'S QUR'AN II
MURDA SEASON II
By **Romell Tukes**
QUIET MONEY III
THUG LIFE II
By **Trai'Quan**
THE STREETS MADE ME III

A Dope Boy's Queen 2

By **Larry D. Wright**
THE ULTIMATE SACRIFICE VI
IF YOU CROSS ME ONCE II
ANGEL III
By **Anthony Fields**
THE LIFE OF A HOOD STAR
By Ca$h & Rashia Wilson
FRIEND OR FOE II
By **Mimi**
SAVAGE STORMS II
By **Meesha**
BLOOD ON THE MONEY II
By J-Blunt

Available Now

RESTRAINING ORDER **I & II**
By **CA$H & Coffee**
LOVE KNOWS NO BOUNDARIES **I II & III**
By **Coffee**
RAISED AS A GOON I, II, III & IV
BRED BY THE SLUMS I, II, III
BLAST FOR ME I & II
ROTTEN TO THE CORE I II III
A BRONX TALE I, II, III
DUFFEL BAG CARTEL I II III IV

Aryanna

HEARTLESS GOON I II III IV
A SAVAGE DOPEBOY I II
HEARTLESS GOON I II III
DRUG LORDS I II III
CUTTHROAT MAFIA I II
By **Ghost**
LAY IT DOWN **I & II**
LAST OF A DYING BREED
BLOOD STAINS OF A SHOTTA I & II III
By **Jamaica**
LOYAL TO THE GAME I II III
LIFE OF SIN I, II III
By **TJ & Jelissa**
BLOODY COMMAS I & II
SKI MASK CARTEL I II & III
KING OF NEW YORK I II,III IV V
RISE TO POWER I II III
COKE KINGS I II III IV
BORN HEARTLESS I II III IV
KING OF THE TRAP
By **T.J. Edwards**
IF LOVING HIM IS WRONG…I & II
LOVE ME EVEN WHEN IT HURTS I II III
By **Jelissa**
WHEN THE STREETS CLAP BACK I & II III
THE HEART OF A SAVAGE I II
By **Jibril Williams**
A DISTINGUISHED THUG STOLE MY HEART I II & III
LOVE SHOULDN'T HURT I II III IV
RENEGADE BOYS I II III IV

A Dope Boy's Queen 2

PAID IN KARMA I II III

SAVAGE STORMS

By **Meesha**

A GANGSTER'S CODE I &, II III

A GANGSTER'S SYN I II III

THE SAVAGE LIFE I II III

CHAINED TO THE STREETS I II III

BLOOD ON THE MONEY

By J-Blunt

PUSH IT TO THE LIMIT

By **Bre' Hayes**

BLOOD OF A BOSS **I, II, III, IV, V**

SHADOWS OF THE GAME

By **Askari**

THE STREETS BLEED MURDER **I, II & III**

THE HEART OF A GANGSTA I II& III

By **Jerry Jackson**

CUM FOR ME I II III IV V

An **LDP Erotica Collaboration**

BRIDE OF A HUSTLA **I II & II**

THE FETTI GIRLS **I, II& III**

CORRUPTED BY A GANGSTA I, II III, IV

BLINDED BY HIS LOVE

THE PRICE YOU PAY FOR LOVE

DOPE GIRL MAGIC I II

By **Destiny Skai**

WHEN A GOOD GIRL GOES BAD

By **Adrienne**

THE COST OF LOYALTY I II III

By Kweli

Aryanna

A GANGSTER'S REVENGE **I II III & IV**
THE BOSS MAN'S DAUGHTERS I II III IV V
A SAVAGE LOVE **I & II**
BAE BELONGS TO ME I II
A HUSTLER'S DECEIT I, II, III
WHAT BAD BITCHES DO I, II, III
SOUL OF A MONSTER I II III
KILL ZONE
A DOPE BOY'S QUEEN I II
By **Aryanna**
A KINGPIN'S AMBITON
A KINGPIN'S AMBITION **II**
I MURDER FOR THE DOUGH
By **Ambitious**
TRUE SAVAGE I II III IV V VI
DOPE BOY MAGIC I, II, III
MIDNIGHT CARTEL I II
CITY OF KINGZ
By **Chris Green**
A DOPEBOY'S PRAYER
By **Eddie "Wolf" Lee**
THE KING CARTEL **I, II & III**
By **Frank Gresham**
THESE NIGGAS AIN'T LOYAL **I, II & III**
By **Nikki Tee**
GANGSTA SHYT **I II &III**
By **CATO**
THE ULTIMATE BETRAYAL
By **Phoenix**
BOSS'N UP **I , II & III**

A Dope Boy's Queen 2

By **Royal Nicole**
I LOVE YOU TO DEATH
By Destiny J
I RIDE FOR MY HITTA
I STILL RIDE FOR MY HITTA
By **Misty Holt**
LOVE & CHASIN' PAPER
By **Qay Crockett**
TO DIE IN VAIN
SINS OF A HUSTLA
By **ASAD**
BROOKLYN HUSTLAZ
By **Boogsy Morina**
BROOKLYN ON LOCK I & II
By **Sonovia**
GANGSTA CITY
By **Teddy Duke**
A DRUG KING AND HIS DIAMOND I & II III
A DOPEMAN'S RICHES
HER MAN, MINE'S TOO I, II
CASH MONEY HO'S
By Nicole Goosby
TRAPHOUSE KING **I II & III**
KINGPIN KILLAZ I II III
STREET KINGS I II
PAID IN BLOOD **I II**
CARTEL KILLAZ I II III
DOPE GODS I II
By **Hood Rich**
LIPSTICK KILLAH **I, II, III**

Aryanna

CRIME OF PASSION I II & III
FRIEND OR FOE
By **Mimi**
STEADY MOBBN' **I, II, III**
THE STREETS STAINED MY SOUL
By **Marcellus Allen**
WHO SHOT YA **I, II, III**
SON OF A DOPE FIEND I II
Renta
GORILLAZ IN THE BAY **I II III IV**
TEARS OF A GANGSTA I II
DE'KARI
TRIGGADALE I II III
Elijah R. Freeman
GOD BLESS THE TRAPPERS I, II, III
THESE SCANDALOUS STREETS I, II, III
FEAR MY GANGSTA I, II, III IV, V
THESE STREETS DON'T LOVE NOBODY I, II
BURY ME A G I, II, III, IV, V
A GANGSTA'S EMPIRE I, II, III, IV
THE DOPEMAN'S BODYGAURD I II
THE REALEST KILLAZ
Tranay Adams
THE STREETS ARE CALLING
Duquie Wilson
MARRIED TO A BOSS... I II III
By Destiny Skai & Chris Green
KINGZ OF THE GAME I II III IV
Playa Ray
SLAUGHTER GANG I II III

A Dope Boy's Queen 2

RUTHLESS HEART I II III
By Willie Slaughter
FUK SHYT
By Blakk Diamond
DON'T F#CK WITH MY HEART I II
By Linnea
ADDICTED TO THE DRAMA I II III
By Jamila
YAYO I II III
A SHOOTER'S AMBITION I II
By S. Allen
TRAP GOD
By Troublesome
FOREVER GANGSTA
GLOCKS ON SATIN SHEETS I II
By Adrian Dulan
TOE TAGZ I II III
By Ah'Million
KINGPIN DREAMS I II
By Paper Boi Rari
CONFESSIONS OF A GANGSTA
By Nicholas Lock
I'M NOTHING WITHOUT HIS LOVE
By Monet Dragun
CAUGHT UP IN THE LIFE I II III
By Robert Baptiste
NEW TO THE GAME I II III
By **Malik D. Rice**
LIFE OF A SAVAGE I II III
A GANGSTA'S QUR'AN

Aryanna

MURDA SEASON
By **Romell Tukes**
LOYALTY AIN'T PROMISED
By Keith Williams
QUIET MONEY I II
THUG LIFE
By **Trai'Quan**
THE STREETS MADE ME I II
By **Larry D. Wright**
THE ULTIMATE SACRIFICE I, II, III, IV, V
KHADIFI
IF YOU CROSS ME ONCE
ANGEL I II
By **Anthony Fields**
THE LIFE OF A HOOD STAR
By Ca$h & Rashia Wilson

A Dope Boy's Queen 2

BOOKS BY LDP'S CEO, CA$H

TRUST IN NO MAN
TRUST IN NO MAN 2
TRUST IN NO MAN 3
BONDED BY BLOOD
SHORTY GOT A THUG
THUGS CRY
THUGS CRY 2
THUGS CRY 3
TRUST NO BITCH
TRUST NO BITCH 2
TRUST NO BITCH 3
TIL MY CASKET DROPS
RESTRAINING ORDER
RESTRAINING ORDER 2
IN LOVE WITH A CONVICT
LIFE OF A HOOD STAR

Coming Soon
BONDED BY BLOOD 2
BOW DOWN TO MY GANGSTA

Aryanna

CPSIA information can be obtained
at www.ICGtesting.com
Printed in the USA
LVHW081514131022
730573LV00011B/310